NAGUIB MAHFOUZ
The Coffeehouse

NAGUIB MAHFOUZ

The Coffeehouse

A NOVEL

Translated by Raymond Stock

The American University in Cairo Press

Cairo   New York

This edition published in 2020 by
The American University in Cairo Press
113 Sharia Kasr el Aini, Cairo, Egypt
One Rockefeller Plaza, New York, NY 10020
www.aucpress.com

Dar el Kutub No. 26767/19
ISBN 978 977 416 999 1

Dar el Kutub Cataloging-in-Publication Data

Mahfouz, Naguib
        The Coffeehouse / Naguib Mahfouz.—Cairo: The American University in Cairo
    Press, 2020
        p.   cm.
        ISBN 978 977 416 999 1
        1. Arabic Fiction—Translation into English
        2. English Fiction—Translation from Arabic
        892.73

1 2 3 4 5   24 23 22 21 20

Printed in Egypt

Abbasiya in its lost youth. An oasis in the heart of a vast desert. In its east loomed mansions like little fortresses, and in its west were small, clustered houses, vain of their hidden gardens and of their newness. On more than one side it was enfolded by green fields, and by forests of date palms, henna plants, and prickly pear trees. Its calm and quiet would have been complete but for the humming of the white tram, shuttling on its well-worn tracks between suburban Heliopolis and Ataba Square. The dry desert wind that beat down, drawing the deepest perfume from the fields, stirred secret love in the breasts of men. And just at sunset, the begging rabab player, wrapped in his long gallabiya, meandered through the streets, barefooted and goggle-eyed, chanting in a rasping voice, but not without a piercing air:

> *I put my trust in you, O Time,*
> *But you returned to betray me. . . .*

❋

Their acquaintance began in 1915 on the playground of the al-Baramuni Primary School. They enrolled at age five and finished at age nine. They were all born in different months in 1910. To this day, they have not moved away from their native district—and will all be buried in the Bab al-Nasr Cemetery. Their group of friends grew to more than twenty as their neighbors joined them. Yet, after some moved to live elsewhere, and others passed away, only five of them have never left each other, the bonds of friendship never slackening—these four, and the narrator. Their closeness in spirit has remained unchanged through the flow of time and all its misfortunes—not even class differences could affect it. This is friendship in all its perfection and all its eternity—the five are one, and the one is five.

1

Two of them were from east Abbasiya, and two from west Abbasiya. The narrator too is from west Abbasiya, but that hardly matters here. Our luck and our destinies have changed over time, but Abbasiya is still our home and Qushtumur still our coffeehouse. Its corners have echoed with our chatter, our laughter, and our tears—and the sound of our heartbeats that have pulsed without end in the beating breast of Cairo.

※

Before we discovered Qushtumur, we used to gather in Hospital Square, by the slender, elegant date palm that stood in the field belonging to Uncle Ibrahim, with Mukhtar Pasha Street on one side, and Between the Gardens Street on the other. Overlooking it were the back lots of many homes in west Abbasiya that filled our need for greenery. The field's south faced a wilderness of thorny fig trees, and to its north, overlooking the district of al-Wayli, a waterwheel turned amid thickets of henna that wafted a sweet fragrance through the air. On our days off school we would sit under the palm towering at its heart, our mouths overflowing with facts and fables. Each pointed out his own house by way of introduction. And so we beheld the home of Sadiq Safwan on Between the Gardens Street, that of Ismail Qadri Suleiman on Hassan Eid Street, and the palace of Hamada Yusri al-Halawani on Hospital Square, along with the villa of Tahir Ubayd al-Armalawi on Among the Mansions Street.

Sadiq and Ismail were amazed by the mansions with their gardens. They were intoxicated with pride to proclaim their friendship with the sons of such distinguished families.

In the evenings their talk was full of information on this world and the next.

"My father's an official in the Ministry of Religious Endowments," boasted Sadiq Safwan al-Nadi—"and my mother is clever in everything!"

With our first sight of Safwan al-Nadi Effendi, he immediately gripped our attention. Short and thin, sporting a long, luxuriant mustache of a kind we'd never seen before, as time passed Safwan Effendi's facial hair became the tempting target of witty remarks, wisecracks, and jokes. Sadiq joined our laughter without reserve, regardless of the love and respect he harbored for his father. As for his mother, Zahrana Karim—whom we called "auntie"—we ran into her sometimes on the street, wrapped in her black shawl. From behind a diaphanous veil she would warn us about the tram as we crossed the road, invoking God for our safety. Sadiq was polite and pious as well: he prayed regularly, and would begin fasting when he reached the age of seven. But he had no brothers or sisters because of an illness that struck his mother during his birth. He was the family's only child, and its enduring hope. We were sure he got lots of care and attention, even though his strict father used to shout at him.

"Sadiq, work hard!" he would bellow. "Your father has nothing to leave you, so make your degree your ticket to getting a job!"

A profound change crept over Sadiq's spirit when he spoke of the world of one of his relations, named Raafat Pasha al-Zayn. He accompanied his father to visit the pasha on Among the Mansions Street, not far from the villa of his friend, Tahir Ubayd al-Armalawi.

"The palace of my cousin, the pasha," he said breathlessly, "is like your family's palace, Hamada. Its garden is nearly as big as Uncle Ibrahim's field—it blooms with all the flowers of this world and the next. And the greeting rooms—the Blue Hall, the Yellow Hall—are huge. The pasha is an awesome man. His wife Zubayda Hanem's beauty has no equal, and she's extremely good-hearted. They love my father and mother as though we are rich like them. Their son Mahmud is older than me by two years, while their daughter Amira is even more beautiful than Zubayda Hanem. Everything there drives you mad!"

Raafat had started out among the minor wealthy, but thanks to Zubayda Hanem's capital, he established the biggest brass factory in the area. God shed his bounty on him in a great many ways. Meanwhile, he set out his traps among the big shots, the elite, and the English—until he procured the rank of pasha.

"Being loaded is the most important thing in the world," declared Sadiq.

The love of lucre took root in Sadiq's heart in the palace of his cousin. This was reflected more in his dreams than in his middling efforts as a student, like most of our group. He was enchanted by Raafat Pasha, Zubayda Hanem, and Amira, who was older than him by seven years: they were the symbols of heaven and its happiness, while he remained an example of the well-behaved believer. If a girl was mentioned, he would fall silent, or else remind us of the torture of the grave and the final judgment.

When his grandfather passed away, Sadiq told us, "Mother said that we are all going to die."

He did not imagine that his mother or father would ever die. There seemed nothing new in what he said, yet we felt secure because death was an eventuality put off until a time unknown. All of us surrender to death with our tongues but in our hearts we toss it aside indefinitely. From time to time it passed near us in funeral processions on their way to the cemetery while we gazed upon them without concern as if these events didn't affect us. We would sit beneath the date palm and play tug-of-war, or feast on the dishes of ice cream studded with biscuits, or mimic the peculiar mannerisms of our teachers.

Nor were we always alone, for dozens of students from the second level would sometimes join us. Some of them were known for their big mouths, coarse language, and love of violent, insolent behavior. Yet our friendship endured as a solid core that would not permit any stranger to enter. Sadiq would invite us to a banquet of a lunch, where he would serve us scrumptious ta'miyya, massive meatballs, and several different kinds of salad, with a platter of oranges and tangerines. On cold, rainy days we would linger until mid-afternoon in his little house on Between the Gardens Street.

Hamada Yusri al-Halawani returned the favor by inviting us to lunch in his palace on Hospital Square. There the beautiful garden welcomed us with its wonderful scents and its gleaming, well-washed greenery. Accompanied by a servant, we made our way to a little, two-roomed house with a balcony that stood alone amid the garden. Through a window that opened upon the garden, the branches danced with a fan-like sway. Spread in every corner of the house were broad leaves glued to sticks that were used to swat flies. For lunch, we had grilled meat, eggplant stuffed with meat and rice, salads, then blancmange for dessert. Before we ate we played tug-of-war without a worry in our heads, and took exercise afterward in the garden's pathways. We watched Tawfiq, Hamada's brother, who was older than him by some years, racing around on a green bicycle. And we glanced furtively at Afkar, his sister of twenty, through one of the palace windows.

Our visit was a happy one, marred only by a single embarrassment. When the silverware was laid out neatly for our meal—knives, forks, and spoons—Ismail Qadri Suleiman made us all squirm when he burst out, "We use just one hand and a spoon!"

Part of Sadiq's praise for the pasha came from the fact that both he and Zubayda Hanem ate as his own family did. Only Mahmud and Amira used their silver.

"Such good people," Sadiq told us. "It's as though they're from us and we're from them. Zubayda Hanem loves salted fish, and my father asked for some as a present. When my mother told her that he's not satisfied until he's eaten onions, Zubayda Hanem served them with the fish."

Sadiq recited this story as though it were a miraculous milestone in the history of human relations. On top of that, he was the handsomest boy among us. Of medium height with light-colored skin, he had a well-chiseled face, deep, dark eyes, and sleek black hair.

❋

We learned a great deal about Hamada Yusri al-Halawani and his family. A royal upbringing in their palace. The pasha owning the biggest tahiniya factory in the country: sweets finer than air and stuffed with pistachio. The palace had a magnificent library, but the pasha had no time to use it. A man of money and business. We saw him a lot going about in his Ford. Of middle height and considerable heft, with a twining mustache and golden-brown skin, he radiated grandeur, as did his wife, Afifa Hanem Badr al-Din. She was not bad looking, but her stateliness overwhelmed her beauty.

5

"Papa is always busy," said Hamada, "and Mama is strict—she likes you to obey. My sister is studying at Mère de Dieu, and my mother has picked out a rich fiancé for her. My brother Tawfiq pleases Mama with his hard work. But she never stops scolding me, and keeps telling me that money has no worth without learning and a home."

"And why don't you apply yourself?" asked Ismail Qadri.

"I like to leaf through the pages of the books in Papa's library and look at the pictures."

"Don't you want to be like your father?" Ismail continued.

"No," said Hamada. "He takes us, my brother and me, to the factory. My brother finds it all fascinating—but I just yawn."

"What you want to be?" Sadiq Safwan asked him.

"I don't know."

His relationship with his family was tense, with the exception of his sister, Afkar. He loved her and said dejectedly, "She's getting ready to leave us."

His father asked him to take heed of his future in the factory, his mother wouldn't cease upbraiding him, and his brother made fun of his laziness. He prayed regularly for a while and then gave it up.

"Only Papa prays all the time," said Hamada.

"And Mama?" Sadiq wondered.

"She doesn't pray. And she doesn't fast. What about Raafat Pasha's wife?"

Sadiq smiled. "She's like your mother, despite her severe nature."

We lost him for a month each year in the summer when his family traveled to Ras al-Barr near Damietta. They were originally from Damietta, and summering in Ras al-Barr was an old local tradition. He told us about their palm-frond hut—and the waves of the sea.

"Are the waves really as high as mountains?" Ismail Qadri wondered.

"Higher!" said Hamada. "And better than that, you can see where the Nile meets the sea!"

This was a bewitching fantasy for those who didn't leave Cairo the whole year round. Even the Armalawis took a short holiday in the country. Hamada was dark-skinned, and his tallness heralded his future

6

growth. His head was large, tinged with nobility and respect. His face was average, but his eyes had a piercing look.

Then, at the end of our days in primary school, approaching age nine, typhoid struck him. He was isolated in a special room; we went to the palace, but were barred from seeing him. He was gone from us for a month, then returned like an apparition. He talked a lot to us about his illness, how he was denied food without even wanting it anyway, then how hunger gnawed at him during his recovery, finally going back and forth between a feeling of starvation and satiety until he nearly fainted. And so he learned through his sickness that everyone truly loved him.

"The whole calamity began with a fly!" he mused.

Even at this early age, we could all see our goals in the distant future. All except Hamada, that is, whose goal seemed obscure.

Tahir Ubayd al-Armalawi, with his simplicity, his lightness of spirit, and his tendency to put on weight, was one of the dearest to our hearts. He was brown-skinned with a common sort of face, but there was no resisting him.

"I'm worn out being an only child," he told us.

"But you have two sisters?"

"I'm the only son. Papa is determined to make me into Egypt's number one medical doctor."

Though less than a mighty mansion, Dr. Ubayd al-Armalawi's villa was nonetheless extremely elegant. The pasha–physician directed the laboratories of the Ministry of Health. He was a man serene in his official grandeur, refinement, and European manner, with a doctorate from Austria. A factotum opened his car door for him. He always appeared to be at the pinnacle, though he was much less wealthy than al-Halawani or al-Zayn. There was a distance about him that set him apart from us. Nor did he welcome his son's mixing with the boys from west Abbasiya, but Tahir avowed to him that he could not cut his relations with his close companions. Our friend's mother, Insaf Hanem al-Qulali, was not only a graduate of Mère de Dieu, like Hamada's mother, but was very cultured and well-read, as well. Thanks to her, the pasha's scientific library was stocked with the fruits of philosophy and the humanities. Both she and the pasha agreed they must make Tahir into a person of the highest stature.

"What are the most treasured study resources you have?" she once asked her son.

"The lines of verse I've memorized," he replied. "For example: *O omen, welcome / To your face I beckon.*"

Even so young he showed a great love of poetry and memorized it as well. Perhaps he found the verse in magazines kept at the villa: he would ask his mother to explain it, then he would instantly memorize it.

All this pleased the pasha.

"The boy is smart—he's going to be an amazing doctor," he told his wife.

Tahir learned about his faith for the first time in the al-Baramuni School. No one mentioned religion, either positively or negatively, at the Villa al-Armalawi. Nor did they practice it in any way: Ramadan and the feasts were religious events only among the servants. In contrast to Sadiq Safwan's great share of belief and religious practice, one could say that Tahir's upbringing was a pagan one, or even without any sort of religion at all. His sisters Tahiya and Hiyam were the same in this respect.

"They both have gorgeous friends who visit them—they sit together in the garden—shining like moons!" marveled Tahir.

He stole away from their meeting, impassioned with an obscure desire. He had received their flirtations like roses. Deep inside him, an innocent, clear, and impulsive delight exploded within him in his first interaction with the opposite sex. One year his family was invited to spend two weeks in Alexandria with his maternal aunt, and we heard about this city the way we had heard about Ras al-Barr. He bathed in the private pool used by the ladies in San Stefano with his mother and his two sisters, and was taken aback by the sight of the hanems in their swimming costumes that looked like nightgowns.

"They were like cows, or even fatter!"

His mother, Insaf Hanem al-Qulali, was of medium build, unlike the style of the time, when obesity was the epitome of beauty, for both women and men. Yet to us it seemed that his first passionate infatuation was with the memorized verses of poetry he recited to us under the palm in Uncle Ibrahim's field. He was enchanted also by cinema: one night we went there for the first time during one of the feasts, at the Bellevue Cinema in Dahir. In truth, it enchanted us all, but he was simply mad for it. That we were only allowed to leave the limits of Abbasiya on holidays only redoubled his passion. Meanwhile cinema occupied an important place in our conversations, and activated our imaginations to such an extent that a cattle ranch turned into our second homeland. The sight of it made our hearts beat faster and filled them with longing.

Ismail Qadri Suleiman too had his say under the date palm. Tawny, strongly built, with honey-colored eyes, a large nose, and an intelligent expression, his small house had a back garden on Hassan Eid Street, and resembled Sadiq Safwan's home on Between the Gardens Street. His father, Qadri Effendi Suleiman, was an official in the railways. Ismail looked like him, except for his bulk.

"My father can ride any train in the country without a ticket," boasted Ismail. "And no one can make cake and meat pies like my mother!"

His four sisters were born before him. Their education had left them just barely literate. They were locked up in the house to prepare them to be housewives. Their looks were middling. In fact, Ismail Qadri was much comelier, yet they married before even turning sixteen, all of them to petty officials in the railways like their father. For the sake of these marriages, their father had sold the only house he owned, in Bab al-Sha'riya.

"As for you, your future is in your own hands," Qadri Effendi Suleiman told his son.

Ismail did not disappoint his father, for he outshone us all at school without any dispute. He studied, memorized, and excelled, never satisfied with either the praise of our teachers or with our amazement. Everyone agreed he was the champion in this field. He was brilliant, loving religion as Sadiq loved poetry, and fasting from the age of seven.

He never stopped imagining God in a majestic form whose grandeur had no limit.

He kept asking the teacher about Him until the instructor grew annoyed and ordered him just to submit and obey. Meanwhile, Ismail had all sorts of entertaining experiences.

"I've been growing onions, watering the crops, and gathering grapes and guava in our little garden," he said. "And I've been hunting frogs to cut open their stomachs and see what's inside."

"Do you want to be a doctor?" asked Tahir.

"Maybe," he said. "I don't know yet."

His reckless curiosity drove him to experiment with an operation on a young female servant's hand, slicing open her palm. At this, his mother became so violently angry that she threatened to perform the same operation on his hand. He burst out crying, begging her not to do it. When his father returned from work and heard what he'd done, he struck him five times with his walking stick. Maybe this was one of the reasons that he later turned away from medicine. Among his most amusing stories were the ones about his visits to his sisters in other parts of the city: he would talk of Shubra and Rod al-Farag, al-Qubaysi and Sayyida Zeinab. His father invited him once for an outing in Luna Park in Heliopolis, and he went along. He grew madly infatuated the same way Tahir did with cinema. He was utterly beguiled by the rides there, like the train and the sliding boat. But the real glory of his childhood was simmering on his rooftop, where he raised rabbits and chickens, and kept a storeroom. In a disciplined manner, he brought the rabbits and chickens food and water, inspected the newborns and gathered up the hens' eggs. In the rooftop room, at his command, clarified butter, whey, cheeses, and molasses were made.

He also covered the wall bordering his rooftop—over which loomed the sky with its birds and stars—with drawings. The room gave him the chance to be alone sometimes. And he had an even more beautiful opportunity when he received the daughters of relatives and neighbors. From that long-ago moment he began his experimentation with religion and with sex. At one instant he would pray, and play husband and wife the next.

His mother was convinced of his piety. She never doubted his seriousness.

"Don't you fear God?" Sadiq Safwan asked him.

He laughed, and—embarrassed—he did not reply. That boy was ahead of us in everything.

We sat on the orchard grass under the date palm, Hamada and Tahir in shirts with short pants, Sadiq and Ismail garbed in gallabiyas. We took great care with our appearance. Hamada and Tahir kept their long hair neatly combed, while Sadiq and Ismail had theirs cropped short. Under the sway of cinema we built up our bodies with games and sports. We took as our highest model the tough-guy hero of the film, be it Tom Mix, William S. Hart, or Douglas Fairbanks Sr. Each of us claimed that his father was a hero, making up stories to prove it: he overpowered a thief that he caught in the house, or beat up a thug who stopped people on the road. Sometimes kids in the streets would pick fights with us, and we, fired by our imaginations, would take up the challenge. Yet the result always dashed our hopes, for those boys fought with head-butts and clogs. When it came to affection, ours for each other was pure and unadulterated. In time we divided into two groups over cinema—one for Le Machiste and the other for the Phantom. The talk would turn furious between us as we lined up to take sides against each other. Still, not one of us uttered an ugly word or made a provocative gesture. Our group incited envy in the hearts of our peers.

11

❋

In 1918, we went to take the entrance exam for the Husseiniya School, as we had finished our elementary studies and reached the age of nine. We waited for the results on the school playground, hoping that misfortune would not split us apart. God be praised, all of us passed. Ismail Qadri did extremely well, while Sadiq and Hamada got by okay; Tahir made it by dint of being the son of Dr. Ubayd al-Armalawi. Thanks to our all being close to the same age, we were all in the same grade—the fourth primary—to which the youngest pupils belonged. New textbooks were given to us, and we carried them—all of them—back home to delight the eyes of our families. Ismail joined the Young Lions football team, then quit it, despairing at his lack of skill. Sadiq tried the drama troupe, but quickly dropped out. Meanwhile, Hamada wanted to be a boy scout, but his parents wouldn't approve. We would meet in the playground for a hasty chat, but outside of school we restricted our gatherings to Thursdays and Fridays. On Thursdays we would go to the Bellevue Cinema, and spend Friday mornings—weather permitting—at the base of the date palm, thus saving our analytical discussions for their former place. Among us, only Ismail Qadri Suleiman felt the urge to excel.

"I heard Papa talking about the three men who went to the English to demand independence for Egypt!" Hamada Yusri al-Halawani confided to us one day.

"That is, for the English to leave Egypt!" he added.

Perhaps we knew no more about the English than that they were our neighbors in Abbasiya, where they kept their barracks. We often saw their soldiers on the trams. For the first time, our families throbbed with this discussion, and the reality arrived at our school itself, with news of the exile inflicted on our leaders. The whole school gathered, all the generations and pupils of various ages, arrayed in different units. We were the youngest group, yet you could find students in the fourth form that already had mustaches! One morning, a group of students sporting hair on their upper lips stepped out of the ranks to shout with thunderous voices, "Strike!" This produced such pandemonium that the overseer of

12

the fourth primary form dismissed us to the care of our professors, and implored the revolutionaries to excuse us from the strike because of our age. Our playground roared with impassioned speeches. Then the pupils surged outside in a stormy demonstration, their first practical lesson in patriotism, which left zeal in our hearts despite our ignorance of what was going on. In our homes we heard echoes of what had happened outside reverberating hotly: it was the first time that fathers and sons met in one burning emotion. Even our mothers were paying attention and were agitated by the swirling events. The December wind that carried tidings of the demonstrations to our houses may have been cold, yet we found it not only warm, but scorching. The deaths of the martyrs were recited like legends. The English patrols ran through our neighborhoods on lorries bristling with weapons, while the crowds' slogans rolled toward us from Husseiniya in the south and Wayliya in the north: "Saad, long live Saad! Total independence or death by violence!"

The news was broadcast in our homes, "Public transport has come to a halt; demonstrations everywhere; the peasants are on the warpath."

The earth trembled unexpectedly, not wanting to calm down. Emotions surged within us, transforming us into new beings entirely. The zeal swept away Sadiq, Ismail, and Hamada—nor was Tahir lacking in it either. Leaflets were handed out, stoking the blazing fire. Something great happened in our quarter when Yusri Pasha al-Halawani was arrested marching in solidarity at the head of the heroes, and we looked at Hamada with admiration.

"Our house is sad, but we are honored," he told us. "If that had happened at any other time, my mother would have died of worry."

But Tahir's relative coolness upset us.

"What about your father?" we asked him.

"Papa is an official," he answered, "one of the ruler's men. Even so, he is with the Revolution, but he . . . ."

"But he *what?*" Hamada pressed him.

"But he has a private opinion about Saad! He doesn't like his past."

Our faces grimaced in protest when Tahir rebuked Sadiq: "Your relative, Raafat Pasha al-Zayn, is one of the ruler's men, too."

13

"That's his own position—he's all by himself," Sadiq rejoined. "We have nothing to do with it."

The fanaticism, the killing and its victims laid a pall over our daily lives, as our little world was enclosed between house and school. And at school, Hamada became a much-loved personality as the son of the imprisoned hero, while each instructor did not hesitate to bestow upon us a nationalist upbringing, regardless of the risk to their own safety and future. Thanks to these great teachers, we learned what had been hidden from us in history since the Urabi revolution. We learned of Saad as a model of power, struggle, intelligence, and righteousness. We grew intoxicated on what we heard, and the spirit of patriotism sprouted within us—which has not been uprooted even today. The country savored its first victory with the release of the exiled leaders—then came the most amazing day when Saad himself returned. Yusri Pasha al-Halawani was freed along with them, and the masses of Abbasiya, Husseiniya, and Wayliya greeted him as he came back to his palace in Hospital Square. Thanks to our friend Hamada's retelling, we were able to visualize the celebration of Saad's homecoming that he witnessed from the place his family had reserved in the Continental Hotel. And we followed the events as a sudden break between Saad and Adly split the revolution's unity. We found Tahir on one side and the rest of us on another, just as we had disagreed before over Le Machiste and the Phantom. But we—despite the division among the leaders—maintained our mutual affection, and our friendship survived.

While the nation was passing from trouble to trouble, and Saad was sent to his second exile, we all reached puberty at nearly the same time. A revolution exploded inside our bodies, warning of impending danger. Ismail Qadri was the only one of us who handled it boldly, taking his sexual daring from the roof of his house to the forest of Indian fig trees in Uncle Ibrahim's field. Meanwhile, Sadiq, Hamada, and Tahir endured the torment of desire in an innocent state of ignorance.

Sadiq Safwan lived in a house blessed with love, harmony, and a stable marital life. As an only child, he was favored with every sort of care—but his adolescent awakening was considered a secret that must be avoided. At puberty, with neither a teacher nor a helper, he abandoned his piety.

"Marriage is the only cure for this," he once told us. "But when will that come?"

Sadiq loved his parents—he was not afraid of them: Tahir Ubayd was like him in this. Safwan Effendi al-Nadi began to escort his son to Friday prayers at the Sidi al-Kurdi mosque.

"Didn't your father's mustache poke those praying on either side of him in the eye?" Tahir teased Sadiq after we'd waited for his return.

Sadiq's father never stopped pushing him to work hard and settle into the right position, for only that would save him from a future of poverty.

"I want to be rich like Raafat Pasha," Sadiq vowed to him.

"Wealth is in God's hand," his father replied. "Your thinking is wrong."

"Didn't he start out on a level close to our own?"

"Don't waste your energy on empty dreams," Safwan Effendi retorted angrily.

"Everyone loves riches," said Ismail Qadri. "But love is one thing, and labor is another."

Raafat Pasha's palace, its people and its splendor, were firmly ensconced in Sadiq Safwan's mind. Their modesty charmed him more than anything in existence. And Amira—despite their difference in age, and even though she was about to get married—no doubt stirred his heart from its innocence. In one way or another, she seduced everyone.

Hamada, the hero's son, kept on growing taller and sleeker. He gleamed like one born into an aristocratic family. He spoke with deliberation, plucking his words from a polished lexicon. He would have held himself aloof from the world in pride—as Mahmud (his actual name, Hamada being his nickname), the son of Raafat Pasha—if he hadn't fallen into our friendship. He never pulled back from this common side for the whole of his life. His sorrow grew worse when his sister Afkar married and moved away from home—she was his only friend on hostile terrain. His brother Tawfiq was favored of status and vague of aspiration. They had lukewarm feelings for each other.

One day Tawfiq told him, "I don't approve of your friends."

"I approve of them—that's all that matters."

Tawfiq sought to stir up the issue with their parents in his presence.

"A man must choose the right kind of companions," he told the pasha.

"All my friends are from the same class to which our leader Saad belongs," Hamada answered him.

The pasha laughed and said nothing.

"Papa wants me to devote my life to the factory," Hamada told us. "Nothing is more annoying than when he urges me to imitate my brother Tawfiq. Yet I do owe his library the happiest hours of my life."

"No doubt your father is a really great reader," remarked Tahir.

"Maybe when he was young," said Hamada. "But nowadays he only relaxes on Sundays."

"What about your mother?"

"She reads newspapers and magazines, and lives in a social whirl."

"So long as you find men like al-Halawani and al-Zayn," said Sadiq Safwan, "then riches are not a pipe dream!"

Then he asked Hamada, "Don't you want to be rich like your father?"

"Of course, I love money," he chuckled. "But I hate the factory."

"Tawfiq will take your father's place after a long while, and become head of the family," said Sadiq. "And what about you? What do you want to be?"

Pausing in confusion, Hamada replied, "I don't know. I still don't love work, but I do love living."

"Tahir loves poetry," commented Ismail.

"Life is more beautiful than poetry, or the factory," Hamada said vehemently.

16

Reflecting for a long time on his elegant appearance, Tahir asked him out of the blue, "Do your parents ever quarrel with each other?"

Taken aback, Hamada asked in return, "What is the meaning of your question?"

"I truly want to know."

"Life is never free of conflict," said Hamada.

"How do arguments between married couples go in your class?"

"Anger flares, they knit their brows," said Hamada, smiling. "My father says, 'Madam, such-and-such is unsuitable,' and Mama says, 'Pasha, I will not hear of that.' It's all 'Madam' and 'Pasha.'"

"Hasn't he ever insulted her by saying, 'Girl, this or that'?" asked Tahir.

"That is your way and not ours, good sir," answered Hamada.

He then told us about his father's greed and his mother's dissipation.

"Papa isn't miserly as Mama sometimes likes to accuse him of being, but he doesn't like to waste a penny without good reason. Mama thinks that good reason includes whatever appeals to her from the goods at Cicurel, including antiques and the food and beverages that she serves at her banquets, as well as gifts for special occasions. She spared no expense to provide my sister Afkar with imported furniture and jewelry. And for the wedding night, she hired Munira al-Mahdiya and Salih Abd al-Hay—the stars of the musical world—to sing."

Guffawing, Hamada added, "Papa told Mama, 'Madam, you are nothing more than a torpedo boat for the British fleet!'"

Nonetheless, the pasha had donated twenty thousand Egyptian pounds to the Wafd. Then he stepped forward at the proper time to take the place of the exiled leaders, and was arrested, joining the line of heroes. He would become a member for our beautiful, vanguard quarter in parliament, and his palace a steady base for the Wafd. But despite all this, Hamada did not match our friend Ismail Qadri either in zeal or loyalty to the Wafd. I told myself that Hamada had not inherited his father's singular virtue in work and holy war. He had acquired his solid build, large head, and lofty brow, a look made for administration and command. But he lacked the fire for either.

❋

Tahir Ubayd belonged to the same class as Hamada, but with his tendency to put on weight and his simple, easy-going attitude, he seemed like one of us. Beneath the date palm we heard his first poetry. Lovingly dutiful to his mother, he set about to learn French, wandering from corner to corner in the palace's great library.

"I'm being pushed," he sometimes told us anxiously. "Woe to me if I don't become an outstanding doctor!"

He was openly bewitched by his two sisters' friends. Finally, Ismail Qadri asked him, "Doesn't your palace have a terrace on the roof?"

"No terrace on the roof and no forest of figs!" he laughed.

Despite having grown up in a half-European villa, he had a vulgar look and attitude. How did he escape shaping by the pasha and his lady? In his parents' eyes, we were responsible for his fall, but he was, in fact, voracious by nature. Not only did he instill in us a love for snacking—a passion for head meat, horse beans, falafel, sausages stuffed with rice and spices, liver, pickled eggplant; sweet couscous, sticky deep-fried treats soaked in syrup, pastries made with flour, clarified butter, and sugar— he also offered them to us using the slang of the streets and alleys, studding his verses with a rebellious vocabulary. We set out on the path to culture with stories written and recited, but he began with the three great poets: Ahmad Shawqi, Hafiz Ibrahim, and Khalil Mutran. And despite the criticism and heavy instruction, he considered primary school the happiest time of his life when it came to his relationship with his parents. He made them happy by learning French, and by memorizing and composing poems. The pasha, though, considered all of this to be at the expense of the profession he had chosen for his son.

"What has poetry got to do with medicine?" he asked, perplexed.

Guided by our instinct for self-preservation, we avoided getting too close to the Villa al-Armalawi and the eyes of the pasha and the hanem. And, in truth, we deserved much of the credit for the blooming of Tahir's popular poetic talent. We dragged him with us to greet Saad as he returned from his second banishment abroad. Our band of friends made up a little

18

wave in the tumultuous sea that seethed in Opera Square. Never in our lives had we seen such a wondrous spectacle, as the turmoil of zeal, the joy of victory, and the force of the tightly packed crowd all swallowed us. Burning emotions—a desire for self-sacrifice, feelings that flew on wings—stole into our hearts over the cares of everyday life. We repeated the cheers for Saad until our throats grew hoarse. Tahir was so intoxicated that he forgot his parents' opinion of the approaching leader. And when the Shaykh's car came into sight with a commanding solemnity as we watched from atop the Ezbekiya Wall with its sweeping view, we all went mad, our limbs alight with a holy fire. Forever stored in the cellars of our consciousness, a day, a memory, and an image that shall never perish! After that date, Abbasiya welcomed days of raucous gaiety. For the first time, we heard of parliamentary elections. We wandered among the tents, listening to the speeches, poems, and electoral doggerel, though the time had not yet come for us to sign up as voters. Through Tahir we heard his father the pasha's view of what was happening around us. He thought, for example, that it was sheer buffoonery that the people chose their leaders in this clownish manner, that we were just imitating Europe without understanding the advances made there and the bases for them. This was in contrast to Yusri Pasha al-Halawani, who proclaimed, in his closing address, that the voice of the people is the voice of God. In reality, however, he was not an eloquent speaker, though the event was filled with orators and versifiers.

At the time that Ubayd Pasha's arrest bestowed on him a halo of grandeur and charisma, Tahir said to his father, "Exile, prison, and confinement, these are what qualify you for battle."

"Governing is knowledge, experience, and aptitude," said the pasha contemptuously, "not exile, imprisonment, and detention."

Meanwhile, Insaf Hanem al-Qulali disdained what was happening no less than her husband.

Ismail Qadri was more or less our leader. That was his right due to his academic excellence, an undeniable distinction. He had a special status among the teachers, not to mention an air of excitement due to his sexual caprices. Since his reaching puberty, his mother had kept a special watch on him, so he lost the opportunities that the roof terrace had offered. Thus he transferred his instinct to the forest of fig trees, into which he lured the daughters of street vendors. Nonetheless, he persisted in his piety like Sadiq Safwan, stuffing his storehouse of information with many things he learned from his mother on the afterlife and the torture of the grave. He sustained his fervor by picturing the image of God.

Finally, one day he said to us, "Maybe He's a bit like Saad, only He wields His authority over the whole universe!"

"Now I know why my father doesn't pray," said Tahir, laughing.

Due to his own humble station, Ismail was happy to gain status with us. He was the only one of these four whose family tree lacked any sort of distinction. Even Sadiq Safwan, who was at a similar level, was closely related to Raafat Pasha al-Zayn. But Ismail had no relatives worth noting. His father had sold the old house he'd inherited when he married off Ismail's sisters. Thus, as we all gravitated toward culture, he used to borrow books to read in his free time from the libraries of Hamada and Tahir. Nothing distracted Ismail from his patriotic feeling and his zeal—so devoted it was almost a religious conviction—for the Wafd. This is what made him move toward law school, enchanted by the law, glory, and politics. Neither medicine nor engineering would satisfy his ambition after Saad Zaghlul became his loftiest model in life.

It was he who incited Tahir against his parents.

"Hearing and obeying should be to people with talent," he said.

No doubt the question that we all asked him so insistently annoyed him: "How can you mix worship and your adventures among the figs?"

"After each prayer I beg God's forgiveness," he once told us. "But what can I do with this blazing fire?"

In the flood of events and passion each one of us prepared himself for the exam to obtain our primary school certificate. All of us passed, Ismail

Qadri in the lead, the rest of us following. We registered at Fuad I Secondary School, where we spent five years, from 1923 to 1928. For the first time we wore long pants as we gave up buying ready-to-wear suits. Years spent in adolescence, learning about cultural refinement and the ways of life. In our first year of study He who Guides led us to the coffeehouse, Qushtumur. A boy called al-Sabbagh, from our broader circle of friends that would gradually fade away, suggested it to us one day.

"The palm tree is no longer an appropriate place for our meetings," he said. "I've found a coffeehouse that is just right for you."

The word "coffeehouse"—which we considered a forbidden thing— frightened us. How could we sit among men our fathers' age, smoking narghilas?

"Don't be scaredy-cats," al-Sabbagh taunted us. "Our fathers got their positions with the same diploma that we earned last summer. The coffeehouse is in an out-of-the way place, at the corner of Dahir with Farouq Street. It's small, new, and beautiful, with a little summer garden. All we have to do is choose a corner in which to talk, play dominoes, and drink tea, cinnamon, and carbonated water."

With great secrecy we groped our way toward Dahir, steered by the spirit of adventure, our consciences assailed by a sense of guilt. Qushtumur appeared to us with its luminous green color, its small size—no bigger than the hallway in the palace of al-Zayn Pasha, as Sadiq exclaimed—and the mirrors mounted on its walls. The little garden, with its four date palms, lay beyond a small, open door. In its center were several square tables. The owner pointed us toward a table deep inside the place, closer to the work counter. We made our way toward it with eyes cast down in deep shame and embarrassment: we were new green shoots, in both age and experience. Three of us came in wearing gallabiyas, and on the shelf behind the counter were narghilas and drinking flagons that redoubled our terror. We sat at the table, meeting withering looks and heated expressions, until a waiter approached us—and so our new ritual began.

This is how we became acquainted with Qushtumur, in late 1923 or early 1924, without knowing that we would bond with it in a marriage

21

that would never split asunder, or that it would instill patience and mutual tolerance in our conversations and our private legends for all of our lives.

At that time we took part in our first patriotic demonstration. We were no longer children safe from punishment, but on the other hand the Interior Ministry was then run by the prime minister, our homeland's leader. From out of the morning's procession the student organizer stepped forward and shouted in a booming voice, "Strike!" The ranks of students rushed toward him eagerly and intently as he harangued them on the crisis between the leader and the king. He called on the people to gather in Abdin Square to show their unconditional loyalty to the leader. The square swelled with humanity of all kinds, as on the day of his return from exile, but this time it seethed with anger. From out of its depths a cry arose, "Saad or Revolution!"

Tahir Ubayd al-Armalawi disagreed with the demonstration, so we left him alone with his opinion. And as we returned, Sadiq Safwan asked us, "But what was the cause of the crisis?"

Clearly we knew nothing. Then Ismail Qadri said firmly, "In any case, we're with Saad, with a reason or without a reason—and against the king, with a reason, or without one either."

In our hearts with agreed with that. In fact, we didn't learn the reasons for the crisis or even care to learn them until many years later when we looked back on the events which had become part of history. In this era we melded with the Wafd in the kiln of its nationalism and were reborn at its hands as new beings.

"There are four religions in Egypt," Ismail Qadri declared one day, "Islam, Christianity, Judaism, and the Wafd."

"And the last one is the most widespread," Tahir answered in derision.

The Wafd taught us what to love and what to hate, and how much to love and how much to hate. The nationalist issue seized us and possessed our hearts, usurping the place of our family, our future, and our personal ambition. We rushed along in the party's flood with identical force and violence, every cell pulsing with the same life and resolve.

Al-Zayn Pasha, al-Armalawi Pasha, and their parties astounded us—were they human, or perversions of nature?

Along with politics, the noble, invigorating winds of culture blew over us, and we devoured the weekly and monthly magazines as well as books, including translations. Beaming lights such al-Manfaluti, al-Aqqad, Taha Hussein, al-Mazini, Haykal, and Salama Musa illuminated our minds. Our talk revolved around ideas the way that it did around politics. Our awakening encompassed the mind, the heart, and the will at once.

Sadiq Safwan, in his piety, drew limits for himself that he could never violate. He loved al-Manfaluti and the other pioneers of Arabic fiction, but he closed off his consciousness before it could affect his belief, or provoke any doubt. If our conversations in Qushtumur exceeded the bounds of tradition then he would retreat into silence, begging God's forgiveness. Meanwhile, his old dream of wealth never weakened, nor his solid admiration for his relative, Raafat Pasha, excepting the political side.

"His politics don't affect our deeply rooted affection," he told us confidently. "He often scolds my father in a gentle manner, asking, 'When, uncle, did you fall for this buffoon?' Or he says to me, 'And you, Sadiq, you follow your father without thinking. Did you really take part in that impertinent demonstration in Abdin Square? I'll bet that you don't know the reason for it. I ask you not to get used to attending demonstrations. They are safe today, but they won't always be that way. How many lives have been lost, sacrificed for that selfish old man?'

"Zubayda Hanem then laughs heartily, and says to my mother warmly, 'Congratulations, Zahrana, your son is a leader from this day on!'"

Sadiq was still enchanted by the pasha, his palace, his antiques, his wife, and his humble character. His infatuation with Amira did not diminish until after she had married and moved away.

"There's nothing wrong with you but your strange dream to be rich!" Ismail Qadri admonished him.

23

"Wealth begins with a dream," said Sadiq.

"Why don't you ask your relation about how to get it?"

"I wanted to do that once," Sadiq admitted. "I motioned to my mother and told her of my thinking—and she warned me it would result in the pasha accusing me of envy."

Sadiq had a completely traditional personality, but he had set a goal for himself that we thought bizarre. As for Hamada al-Halawani, like the others he had opened the windows to culture without reserve. He would insist on reading to us at night what he had read the day before, a dazzling, magical, believable novel that he would take upon himself the trouble to critique.

"Culture is a lethal assault, inciting us against abuses."

And if his latest reading was on religion, he would summarize it in a lofty tone, then tell us with certainty, "This is the defining word on the faith."

The discussion came from clashing sides. At the beginning, Hamada had no deep-seated beliefs and suffered no real crisis. At times we'd hear him say, "This is the story of humankind, and this is its origin."

Then he would happen to read a moderate book on religion and science, and adjudge, "It seems there is no contradiction between faith and knowledge."

What he learned profoundly influenced him, and he quickly shifted from one stance to another. He defied any definition or description. One night he'd be a liberal, the next, a socialist.

"But what are you?" Sadiq queried him.

"There's a long road ahead of me," he replied, perplexed.

Tahir Ubayd, on the other hand, seemed to have a clear objective and perspective. None of us doubted his poeticism. He memorized poetry, savored it, and began to compose it. He loved colloquial folk poetry as well: at first he recited to us verses for wooing his sisters' girlfriends, then a thousand pieces making fun of the mustaches of Sadiq's father, Safwan Effendi al-Nadi. He drank in the writings of the pioneers, and did not want in his studies of the great modern poets, or selections from the works of Abu Tamam al-Buhturi.

"Soon I'll be reading in French," he told us.

Modern culture added little to his beliefs. He had been raised more or less without religion, a subject that neither aroused his interest nor occupied his mind. But he was fascinated by people, beauty, and song. His conscience was built on lofty values. Having grown up in the Villa al-Armalawi he was detached from the magical side of Saad Zaghlul, yet neither was he bound in loyalty to the king. When the party squabbles broke out, they filled him with loathing and disbelief in them all.

"Egypt deserves love," he pronounced, "but she hasn't found anyone yet who loves her for herself."

Ismail Qadri did not read as much as Hamada. But he did think about what he read and would discuss it with us.

He expressed a particular viewpoint when he told us, "Modern culture is massing for an attack on the fortress of religion and tradition."

He explicated further by saying, "It begins with fables: these become widespread and are used to answer the great questions."

"Has doubt begun to whisper in your breast, too?" Sadiq Safwan asked anxiously.

Ismail gazed at him meditatively for a long time.

"Thought has no boundaries," he said at last.

"Allow me to congratulate you!" Tahir interjected, giggling.

"Religion is one thing," Ismail replied, scowling. "God is another."

"Listen to the wonder," said Sadiq, slapping his palms together.

Evidently he thought and he doubted, but he would not surrender his skepticism except to the Wafd. He was more inclined toward general learning than he was to art or literature. Regarding the future, he focused on the law, considering it the gateway to glory and politics. We believed in him and trusted in his reaching his ultimate goal. And at the time that culture became the objective in the life of Hamada al-Halawani, it was an essential foundation in the life of Ismail Qadri, over which he built his towering edifice. He was a man of action, not the pen. His dreams were heralds of his deeds. He moved along steadily and surely, despite his poverty and lack of high position or influence.

25

✻

With culture flared the burning fire of desire. Crueler than doubt and more stubbornly insistent, it pursued us both day and night. The fair sex pulled eyes away from magazines whenever it loomed at a window or strolled on the street. The gaze would be lost in the faces and the shapes of the bodies that beat with life through the loose, flowing garments. Ismail remained a locus of envy, yet he suffered no less than the others.

One day al-Sabbagh came to us and asked, "Have you seen this book?"

According to the outer cover, this was a work of history. But that concealed its real title, *The Return of the Shaykh*. We decided to read it discreetly, exchanging it with one another. We quickly scanned its chapters to grasp the gist of its famously ribald stories. Our fires raged more fiercely and leapt even higher with the demons' kindling. And when al-Sabbagh was sure that we'd lost our grip on reason, he began to talk about the prostitutes' district.

"Does the government know about it?" Sadiq asked in confusion.

"The government provides the license and protects the place's security," he said, sounding like an expert.

That Thursday we turned away from the Bellevue Cinema for Clot Bey Street. Al-Sabbagh led the way and we followed after him, astonished at our goal and in terror of the result. These old houses whose foyers were adorned with women of all shapes and colors . . .

"It's so crowded!" whispered Hamada.

"Let's hurry back before there's a scandal!" urged Sadiq.

"Does anyone of you expect to meet his father here?" al-Sabbagh said mockingly. "Every client here is on his own. Go on, don't be cowards—make up your minds quickly."

We found that vanishing into one of the houses was easier than lingering amid the crowds. Later we met at the start of the street, exchanging blanched looks. We remained silent until we had gathered at our table in Qushtumur. Each was impatient to know what had happened with the others.

The first to confess was Sadiq Safwan.

"The first time, and the last," he said.

"Why?" someone asked.

"From the standpoint of beauty, there was nothing wrong with her," he explained. "The room had a floor of stone blocks. The bedclothes, the mirror, and the couch were all antiques. She pointed toward a metal plate on the couch, and said crudely that I should put the money in it. So I did as she asked. As soon as I had, she took off her red dress and was left completely naked. She then gestured with her hand to show she was in a hurry. I immediately cooled, as if I had never felt any lust at all. 'I'm sorry; thank you,' I told her politely, 'but I'm leaving.' So she said, 'Go in safety.' I seek refuge in God—but that was the first and last time."

We laughed so hard that we relaxed. This encouraged Tahir, who told us of his adventure.

"I found a peasant girl with a tattoo on her chin and a smile on her face. I headed toward her and she beat me to the stairs. I didn't care about the room. She said to me, 'You're like a mule despite being so young.' I laughed and laughed, but I was upset. I cooled off the way that Sadiq did. I felt very strange, and quickly changed my mind. 'Excuse me,' I told her, 'I'm not ready this time.' So she said, 'You're free to do what you want, but you still have to pay.' So I paid up the piasters and rushed toward the door, as she said to me, 'You've got a bottom I'm tempted to smack,' and I scrambled even faster for the exit, like one making a getaway."

We laughed for a long time at this. Then Sadiq asked, "The first and the last time?"

But he didn't reply.

"A successful venture, thanks to good fortune," said Hamada al-Halawani. "Her eyes pleased me. She was very polite and encouraging; she let me embrace her as we were standing upright, and it was all done very quickly. Everything was fine!"

All eyes now lighted on Ismail Qadri. As he was the only one of us who had prior experience with sex, we expected the best results from him. He laughed more than he usually would, as he told us:

27

"My girl was young and her body was not bad. When we went into the room together, in came a woman between forty and fifty years old. She had a massive build and a powerful personality. The young one scurried over to her and they whispered together, probably about the job, then the madam left the room. Suddenly I felt an overwhelming desire for the matron, who still seemed young herself. So then I told the girl, 'I want the madam.' She was shocked. 'She's the boss, she isn't like that,' she said. I asked her to grant my wish—she hesitated for a bit, then went out. Before I knew it, the madam came back and locked the door behind her. 'Pay me double,' she croaked in a rough voice. 'I only have ten piasters,' I told her. But she didn't refuse, and when I drew her toward me, my arms couldn't reach all the way around her. I enjoyed it to the limit."

"You're not a normal person," hooted Tahir Ubayd.

Al-Sabbagh stopped seeing us for one reason or another—but we never stopped going to Clot Bey Street. Sadiq Safwan was the only one of us who didn't repeat the experience, as the whole district aroused his disgust, agreeing neither with his religion nor his taste. Tahir didn't stay away, but he typically would sit in a low-class coffeeshop listening to Arabic songs and staring at the people going by. As for his view of the area, he put it this way:

"This exhibition of women and men is totally evil and crazy: its devotees must have lost their minds before ever going there."

With politics, culture, and sex, love also dawned on us, with all its light. The first of us to become drunk on its pure elixir was Sadiq Safwan. When he first saw Ihsan in the company of her mother, Fatima, as they left their home on Abu Khoda Street, our friend was sixteen, and the girl thirteen. Every time we passed near their residence on our way to Qushtumur, he raised his eyes over two worried cheeks to the window on the second floor. Ihsan was a great deal riper than her years: a full, graceful body; a round, fair-skinned face; luxurious chestnut hair; honey-colored eyes; and a perfectly formed mouth—a shape commonly called "King Solomon's ring." It was clear to everyone that she was attracted to him, or at least she was attracted to his attraction to her.

"The girl is like an apple," Sadiq told us ecstatically. "And she's so lively. We've found out that her father was called Ibrahim al-Wali, a petty government employee with a lot of children."

"Have you now learned what love is?" asked Tahir Ubayd.

"I'm dazzled by her lightness of being," said Sadiq. "The world spins when my gaze meets hers. Every time I think of her I feel an amazing happiness."

"I felt something like that about Mary Pickford," offered Tahir. "And something similar for my sisters' friends in the past."

"You haven't loved yet," replied Sadiq.

"I control myself thanks to the fig tree forest, Clot Bey Street, and my dedication to work," said Ismail Qadri. "I'm seeing a neighbor's daughter, but I have no patience for letting my work slide or for standing at a window."

Hamada al-Halawani turned toward Sadiq.

"You are in love. So what's next?" he inquired.

"Hold on," he cautioned, "I haven't succeeded yet."

Tahir Ubayd stirred us with his poetry before exciting us with his love life. He came to us when he published his first courtship poem, called "The Belles in the Garden," in *Intellect Magazine*—a well-established, widely distributed periodical, known for its call to the spirit of the age. This was recognition in every meaning of the term. Our little corner of Qushtumur shook with delight and rapture on the occasion.

"We are witnessing the birth of a poet," Hamada declared with pride.

"Do your parents know you published it?" Sadiq asked breathlessly.

"Within the sphere of our villa, my talent pleases my parents—they regard it as preparation for ophthalmology, my talent kept in reserve," said Tahir. "But my father grimaced when he saw my poem in the verse section of *Intellect Magazine*. 'This is literary work,' he told me furiously, 'it is not suitable for your status.' I answered, 'Shawqi Bey was a poet, Papa.' But he said, 'Shawqi was, first and last, a prince of the royal court. But poetry itself is a beggars' profession.'"

In any case, this didn't ruin his happiness over his poem's publication. Ismail Qadri recommended that he pay a visit of thanks to the magazine, to strengthen his acquaintance and his ties to it—and so he did. There he gained new collegial relations with, and learned the progressive values from the cream of those who believed in them. He empathized with the avid will to destroy the old world entirely and to built a new one based on modern science. It was as though he wanted to exterminate, with the old world, his father's gloomy ideas. Yet his empathy did not go beyond friendship to this principle and its adherents without committing himself to its ideals or adapting his behavior. At this time he emerged from his cocoon of pure, passionate love into the fray of a genuine experiment. One day Sadiq saw him waiting in front of the Abbasiya Pharmacy to watch Raifa Hamza as she walked out of it. She was a nimble, brown-skinned girl with fine features, an exciting body and breasts, and who was at least Tahir's own age. Virtually no one in Abbasiya was unaware of her, for she lived with her mother in an apartment in a not-very-old building that looked out over our quarter on one side and the great medieval cemetery on the other. Raifa was a nurse, practicing the pharmacological profession of giving injections to the sick; it was said that she also worked in a hospital. She was held in bad repute without any basis, but that's how things went in Abbasiya. So long as she worked by going nimbly from house to house with a comely face and a plain dress, she had to be disreputable. Tahir was her polar opposite, with a body that leaned toward obesity and a dreamy expression. Who did not know Tahir, son of Ubayd al-Armalawi Pasha? He smiled when she turned away from him—he did not get angry. He continued the chase as hope loomed before him. Thus there were two lovers in our meeting of friends: their states of mind revealed the temptations of magic and ecstasy.

"Raifa needs a safe place—I mean, a private apartment, for example," Hamada al-Halawani told Tahir.

"I know what she needs," said the experienced Ismail Qadri, "but you'll have to spend more money."

"It's as if you two are talking about a prostitute!" exclaimed Tahir.

They both fell silent in surprise.

"I'm sorry, both of you, but you know what people are saying. . . ."

"Nonsense," said Tahir. "I love Raifa just as you love Ihsan."

What he said made everyone hold their tongues, despite their inner whisperings. Then he picked it up again.

"I approached the matter in the wrong way from the start," he said. "I followed her from house to house without result. It became clear to me that she was a hard worker, who did nothing but perform her task and then go home. People's tongues are unforgiving; they slander people without any proof. In truth, when she smiles at me, new feelings invade me, and I know that I'm in love with her."

After they got to know each other, they promised to meet in the Birbis Gardens.

"One has to be dedicated," she told him. "I serve a noble profession. People's tongues are so vile."

"Maybe some of us thought that she's a wily girl and I'm a nice boy, a fine poet of good family who has no experience in the cunning of the alleys," said Tahir. "Bring me one piece of evidence against her," he challenged.

Actually, none of us ever caught her on an empty street with another man, or heard anything specific against her. We wished our friend well.

They exchanged symbolic gifts. Once, when he was drunk with love, he told us, "I'm determined to go to the lawful end with her."

Then, after a pause, he resumed, "She knows my family and appreciates my circumstances: once she asked me, as a precaution, 'Are you able to stand up to them?' I told her that I could handle anything."

We were justifiably confused by this great transformation.

"You're only sixteen," Hamada al-Halawani reminded him.

"Marriage has its own proper time," he replied.

"The proper time for her is different," said Hamada.

"Love doesn't recognize that," laughed Tahir.

"Does she understand you as a poet?" Ismail Qadri queried him.

"At least she doesn't misunderstand me," he answered. "What I really admire is the strength of her personality."

"Would you split with your family because of her?" asked Hamada.

"That doesn't worry me."

"Have you now learned what love is?" Sadiq teased him.

"Maybe it's madness or a sickness," he chuckled. "But regardless, it's the peak of happiness."

"And Mary Pickford? And the dalliances in the garden?"

"Those were appetizers."

"Is it different from sex?" Ismail Qadri asked with interest.

"It's an angelic tree whose fruit seeds are sex."

Then Sadiq confessed to us, "I asked my mother if she would read the Fatiha with Fatima, Ihsan's mother. My father thought it over for a while and did not object."

Hamada al-Halawani—influenced, perhaps, by his conversations with the two lovers—fell into the trap of love himself. We learned that he was infatuated with Samira al-Ma'ruqi.

"She has everything you could want," he told us. "She is a girl of sixteen too, from the middle class. She visits the neighbors unveiled and by herself: she is considered westernized. She used to do that with her parents, despite the objection of her paternal cousin who was jealously guarding the family's reputation."

Of course, Hamada was well known as the scion of the very wealthy nationalist hero, Yusri Pasha al-Halawani. Through her female servant, he invited her to a rendezvous on Among the Mansions Street, which became a lovers' lane by night.

From the start, we thought that Hamada had plunged into a unique adventure, but had not yet been afflicted with the true love that had burst into the hearts of Sadiq and Tahir. In any case, they met on the road of love, but the experiment was aborted before it began. They had hardly been together for a few minutes when her paternal cousin swooped down upon them like a ferocious beast. He slapped the girl on the face so hard that she lost her balance and fell to the ground. He then assaulted our friend verbally until a policeman noticed them. The scandal spread from mouth to mouth, kicked about like a football. Yusri Pasha was livid with rage.

"He attacks you and here I am, standing here with my hands tied, because we are the transgressors," he fumed. "How would you behave with girls from good families? And who is this al-Ma'ruqi, anyway? What a disappointing child you are."

Our companion won contusions on his cheeks and lips from the battle, and was grounded for a number of days in the palace. When he came back to us, we couldn't help but laugh at him.

"What are you up to?" Tahir asked eagerly.

"Nothing," he answered coolly.

"Don't you love her?"

"Everything perished in the battle," he quipped.

"Didn't you exchange any words?"

"We just said hello and declared our attraction to each other—then what happened happened."

"Maybe she's waiting for another move on your part?"

"Nothing new will happen."

"The problem is that you weren't in love," opined Sadiq Safwan.

"Maybe," he shrugged.

Ismail Qadri did not veer from his path.

"Sex is a great and famous thing, in and of itself," he said bluntly.

"A strange view for someone of your culture and intelligence."

"Sex is what brings you into existence. It doesn't bother me when al-Manfaluti says, 'Maybe he was distracted from love, or wasn't made for it.'"

In the deluge of private preoccupations, the nation's heart throbbed deeply and painfully at the death of the leader, Saad Zaghlul. We were left dumbfounded, our souls burning with the sense of loss and bereavement. Even Tahir Ubayd was despondent and regretful, for the deceased's leadership had overshadowed all in the nationalist coalition: his adversaries loved him like his disciples and followers. Each one of us had a story of how he'd heard the report with his family, and how much the tears flowed. Every eye wept for Saad, every heart was filled with grief.

"How did Ubayd Pasha and Lady Insaf take the news?"

"Sadly, of course," answered Tahir. "My father told me that in his last years, he'd made up for his past entirely, and had become a father to the people and the patriotic movement."

Our group went together to Opera Square, squeezing into the scowling, mourning crowd, and waiting. When the coffin appeared, mounted on the caisson, shrieks of agony rose in the clear August sky that dripped with heat and humidity. We were swept along with the flow of people behind the funeral cortege to Muhammad Ali Street. There the shouts mixed with the wails of the women watching from their balconies. We returned to Abbasiya silent, without Saad. We plunged into new waves of our history overflowing with heat and anxiety. We swore our allegiance to Saad's successor, and watched the harbingers and portents that appeared in the heavens.

And in the year of the baccalaureate, we redoubled our purpose to finish, with success. Ismail Qadri worked very hard to excel and to enroll in the school of law without tuition. But misfortune blocked his path with a wily conceit. For at the end of the first trimester of the academic year, heart disease forced Qadri Effendi Suleiman to stay in bed. Distraction with his father's ordeal wrecked the order of Ismail's life, as the family's woes multiplied from the cost of doctors and medicine. Ismail spoke to us about his father's illness—about his frailty and the swelling in his legs, and the feeble hope for his recovery—with intense distress. And indeed, Qadri Effendi never regained his health: he gave up the ghost near the end of March, about a month before the exam. His sickness and death left our friend inconsolable. Ismail was awarded his degree but ranked lower than he deserved. His father's pension did not meet his expenses: it was hardly enough to cover his family's basic needs.

"There's no chance for free enrollment now except in the Faculty of Arts," he said dejectedly, when someone asked what he would do.

"Don't be sad," said Sadiq soothingly. "You could be superior in any field you enter."

"What a fateful blow!" lamented Ismail in surrender.

As for the rest of our friends, Tahir went to the School of Medicine, as his father insisted.

"By itself, your passing the exam, without any effort by me on your behalf, would not have qualified you for medical school," the pasha told him. "Yet you could have excelled on your own if you had resolved to do so."

"But I'm a poet, Papa!"

"Even acknowledging the fact that you bear this defect," retorted his father, "that shouldn't prevent you from studying medicine. I know doctors who are mad like you, but they're physicians just the same."

"Can you study medicine despite yourself?" asked Hamada al-Halawani.

"Let's forget a medical career and the way to get there," said Tahir. "The most important thing is that *Intellect Magazine* hails my poetry, and its editor is always urging me to produce more of it. The decisive battle with my father is looming, and there's nothing wrong with that."

Hamada al-Halawani entered the school of law without wanting to study that or anything else.

"I did it to keep my father quiet—no other reason," Hamada assured us. "He's now given up trying to tempt me to take an interest in his work, and is satisfied that my brother Tawfiq will take over from him. I went to the school of law to convince him that I too have a serious goal."

"You could well be a prosecutor or a judge," Sadiq told him.

"My goal is greater than that," he rejoined. "I'm enamored with culture, life, and freedom."

"Freedom?"

"Call it 'unemployment' for now, if you will," said Hamada.

As time passed, his dream began to crystallize and take solid form. He lived like an aristocrat, plucking a flower from every garden, ranging both far and wide, in spirit and in the flesh, without ties or obligations.

"He's capable of realizing his dream," marveled Ismail Qadri.

The really shocking surprise crashed in on us from the direction of Sadiq Safwan. His handsome face lit up with glee, as he told us, "I have a bomb for you!"

We paused with anticipation, to set the mood.

"I'm going to open a novelty shop!" he blurted.

Had the mild-mannered, religious youth gone mad? But it was true. He explained to his parents that he had decided not to complete his education, and to open the curio shop as a first step on the way to wealth. Safwan Effendi was incredibly upset: Zahrana Karim believed that an evil eye had harmed her only son.

"You must be joking," his father pleaded.

"I'm absolutely serious."

"You've gone absolutely mad!"

"Why, Father? I'm sane, and I know what I want."

"Before you, I've never heard of a literate person who preferred to own a shop rather than be a government employee."

"Compare the minimum amount of profit from the shop with the salary of any official."

"Money isn't everything," his father reprimanded him. "The butcher is a rich man!"

"Money is the most important thing."

"And dignity?"

"Honorable work grants dignity," riposted Sadiq.

"Pampering has spoiled you," replied his father. "This is the problem. And where have you got the experience to do this work?"

"We have friends of every kind," he said calmly and politely, to soothe his agitation. "Some of them are grocers, and some are curio shopkeepers."

"That isn't enough!" his father barked in rage. "Where will you get the money to start it with?"

"There is a shop for three pounds in the new building that stands between Abbasiya and Abu Khoda. Mother owns some old jewelry: I will get double its worth back for her."

"Here's my opinion," said his father. "Children's thoughts and child's games."

The happy ending came from an unexpected quarter. During a family visit to the palace of Raafat al-Zayn, Safwan complained about his son to the pasha.

36

"Bravo!" Raafat shouted, to Safwan's great surprise.

"Bravo, my dear pasha?" Safwan asked, confused.

"Sound thinking," said the pasha. "The world must always change: do you know that it will be the only novelty shop in all of Abbasiya?"

The man's agitation ceased. "Doesn't every project require the right financing?" he ventured.

"That's true," the pasha answered. "The plan must be a strong one. I'll lend him what he needs without interest, and cover his steps."

Safwan Effendi's opposition ended on the spot. Zubayda Hanem began to tease the boy, chuckling, "Blessed you are, Uncle Sadiq!"

The child's play turned into serious business, as we looked on, incredulous. The shop was rented, and the pasha sent a man from his circle to organize the shop, hire the right carpenter, take control of Sadiq's books, and teach him the tricks of the trade. The pasha also introduced him to wholesale dealers that he knew, and vouched for him to them. And before the end of the summer and the start of university, Sadiq was strutting cockily in his shop amid shelves crammed with tissue paper, beverages, cigarettes, shaving equipment, bits of embroidery, various kinds of chocolate, sticky sweets with pistachios, cucurbit seeds, and peanuts. We should have adjusted to the new situation and treated it as seriously as it deserved, but at first, it seemed to us like a game or an act. We would stroll past him, trading smiles with each other, watching him stand behind the wooden partition or handle an order; we saw his customers, young boys, girls, and ladies. He was perfectly business-like—even his mustache had started to sprout. Fortunately, it did not grow gigantically like his father's, but confined itself to his upper lip, like Charlie Chaplin's.

After the shop had closed for the night, he would catch up with us at Qushtumur, emigrating to the world of culture and politics. Ismail Qadri exulted in the number of his customers from the fair sex. Hamada commented on that by reciting the local proverb, 'God befriends he who is without friends,' and asked him with great interest about the profits.

"I'm paying off my debt to the pasha first," said Sadiq. "Yet what's left for me is what a young employee cannot dream of."

It wasn't long before he dropped another bomb among us.

"I'm planning to get married without delay," he told us one night.

This time we were not amazed, as we knew how religious and virtuous he was. To our inattentive ears, the voice of the bygone age was clear in the crush of events and the ceaseless flow of the seasons. Some of us sat in on the university amphitheater while one of us enthusiastically sought to perfect his faith. Sadiq decided to announce his wish, then asked his new family to wait until he could raise the appropriate sum.

It appeared that Ibrahim Effendi al-Wali wasn't amused by the boy's turning from effendi to novelty merchant. But Safwan Effendi told him with pride, "My son has earned a baccalaureate. Haven't you read what the intellectuals have written about books with liberal ideas?"

Ihsan genuinely, decisively, and unequivocally agreed, and each family set about preparing for the happy day from its own side.

"What's the hurry?" asked Safwan Effendi. "It was better that you wait until you had repaid your debt. Then you could economize with care until you could own a house that was proper in every respect. Let's not forget that Ibrahim Effendi al-Wali is a formidable man, and God does not charge a soul to do something beyond his ability."

Yet Sadiq reassured his father that things were going very well indeed. Meanwhile, we learned the reason for his haste and why he was so anxious about the promised day.

"It's going to be a tremendous battle without mercy—and may the Lord forefend," said Hamada, laughing.

Sadiq rented a three-roomed apartment in the building overlooking his shop. His mother sold her old jewelry to cover the dowry and the engagement gift. When this happened, Raafat Pasha told Sadiq within his parents' hearing, "Zubayda suggested to me that we let you off the rest of your debt, but I refused. I want you to build yourself up on your own efforts, not with handouts from anyone."

Yet he gave him beautiful furniture for his sitting room, including a couch and two armchairs, plus a set of china and kitchen utensils too. He furnished the apartment with simple things, but they were, naturally, new, with a special smell that lingered for a long time in Sadiq's senses.

On the night of the wedding, we gathered in the little pavilion on Abu Khoda Street. We sat with the invitees in serried rows, watching Safwan Effendi with his slight body and mammoth mustache. From the platform, Abd al-Latif al-Banna gazed down on us with his traditional Arab orchestra, as he sang for us a light, saucy song:

"Let the house's curtain fall
So your neighbors can't see all:
What happy folks are we!"

Sadiq appeared, confused between the building and the pavilion, greeting us ebulliently. He hid an inner bewilderment behind a pleasant smile.

"We'll eat dinner at a private table," he told us.

"I've got a private bottle in my pocket that I've smuggled along with me," said Hamada al-Halawani. "Tonight, everything for me is permitted."

"We're responsible for you until the cock crows," said Tahir.

Raafat Pasha didn't go to the tent, but our friend informed us that he had visited the family to congratulate them, and that his wife had stood out, like the full moon in her beauty, among the society of women. The groom asked that we watch the wedding procession with him. He sounded us out, but the effort failed. Those in charge would not tolerate the presence of strange young men among the female invitees.

"How perplexed and frightened he seems," said Hamada.

"The matter is decisive and dangerous, and will not get any better," said Tahir.

We each wondered when our day would come, and how it would be. We all breathed anxiously with pleasure and curiosity. On the return to our homes we pictured our friend in a state of undress, his apprehension and embarrassment lengthening as he waited for her at the approach of his dream.

He was absent from us for a whole week. During his first time back with us in Qushtumur, we rained questions down on him in a siege strengthened by repressed desires, until he felt compelled to make a confession.

"I didn't have more than a single glass," he told us. "That was not merely enough, but more than enough. We had no sooner shut the door upon ourselves when I felt that I had been freed from the burdens of life, from traditions, ghosts, restrictions, and bans. I felt I had to liberate her from the crown of jasmine laid around her head, and drew her to my chest. Then the pleasure of being fled in the turmoil of a strange embarrassment mixed with exhilaration in a brain that could not withstand the effusions of the fiery glass. I confessed to her that my head was spinning, and she allowed me to fall back and relax. So I did, and spent the rest of the night in a state between waking and sleeping. Then I awoke, and my senses awoke too. I roused her from her slumber with kisses, and . . . what can I say? Your brother is a lion!"

Then Sadiq laughed in a clear, affecting way, "We were both on fire—nothing could put us out."

We listened raptly as he told us how he had been repressed and confused, with an old, frustrated urge. She was light of spirit, as her abundant liveliness declared. For this was their honeymoon, brimful with honey. He returned to his shop after a vacation of a whole three days. He took up his work on his own, after the man sent by Raafat Pasha had completed his mission to train him, and the shop had become a meeting place for people coming and going. That this was the only curio shop around was itself a master stroke. The lack of shops in Abbasiya was due to its residential areas being divided into two separate spheres: palatial mansions in the east and villas in the west. The only shops were those that appeared when a house was torn down and a building arose in its place. With all his being, Sadiq was preoccupied with love and confidence. As for politics and culture, these he had banished to the margins of his life.

"There's no room for reading in your life right now," said Hamada al-Halawani.

"The newspaper at most," replied Sadiq. "And I might read an article in a magazine."

Meanwhile, the nation fell into a series of surprising events. The coalition broke up and Muhammad Mahmud put together a new cabinet, suspending the constitution. Then came the conflict between the Wafd led by al-Nahhas on one side, and the king, Muhammad Mahmud, and the English on the other. Ismail Qadri was the most emotionally affected by all this among us. He had always been a fanatic—in politics, culture, and sex. Hamada's excitement and passion were both immeasurably less than his, despite his father the pasha being one of the stars of the conflict. Ismail took part in all the student demonstrations, while Sadiq confined himself to declaring his displeasure, and Hamada did not go to protests outside the university's walls, as though he was above any mixing with the masses. Tahir stuck to a seemingly neutral position: he would not proclaim his allegiance to his family's point of view, nor did he join the other side.

"Let whoever will solve the problem solve it," he told us one day. "If it's not Mustafa al-Nahhas, then it will be Muhammad Mahmud."

Then one day he remarked on something we hadn't considered before.

"Don't you think," he said, "that the Wafd is progressive politically and reactionary intellectually, while the Liberal Constitutionalists are reactionary politically and progressive intellectually?"

In fact, in culture we did not differ as Wafdists or Liberal Constitutionalists, nor did our political passions influence our appreciating merit in our opponents. Indeed, were we not charmed by some English writers, though England was our enemy?

To the extent to which our friends' liberated cultural lives were favored with brilliant progress, boldness, and bloom, their university studies crept along with an alarming lassitude that warned of failure. Hamada took his legal lectures coolly and with nonchalance. Ismail Qadri saw himself as banished to the Faculty of Arts to earn a degree he did not love in order to buy a job that he hated.

"You have the potential to be a great professor," Sadiq said to encourage him.

"If a person's goal becomes impossible, then death may conquer him."

But Tahir persevered in publishing his beautiful poetry, establishing his feet firmly in *Intellect Magazine*, where he began to translate selections from French works, as well. From its side, the magazine offered financial rewards that brought him limitless good fortune and which he squandered on us in the most delightful manner.

We warned him of the coming battle with his parents.

"Let the combat begin!" he laughed.

"Console your parents by succeeding, then do what you want with yourself afterward," said Sadiq.

"I don't like slavery," he declared insistently.

At the close of the academic year, Hamada and Ismail passed, but Tahir failed completely. A genuine crisis erupted in the Villa al-Armalawi. Their hope was extinguished in the heir-apparent, who sat accused in the defendant's cage before Insaf Hanem and the pasha.

"This score belongs to another person, that is for sure," said the pasha with deep morosity.

"Given your intelligence, you had a great responsibility," Insaf reproached him. "We want to know how you interpret it."

His heart overflowed with agony, but he was too big to surrender his soul.

"I entered medical school unwillingly, that's how I interpret it," said Tahir.

"You're not a child," said his father. "What is it you want?"

"My future is with poetry and journalism," he told them.

"That is very bad news," replied the pasha.

"The matter is very simple, Papa."

"What you have in mind is going to create another catastrophe."

"Oh what a disappointment!" his mother moaned, her head in her hands.

"I'm very sorry," he said. "But I have no choice."

He finished telling us his story by saying, "The villa is like a mourning tent, and I'm totally upset."

"You won't reconsider?" Sadiq asked him.

"Soon I'll sign up with the magazine as a poet and a translator," answered Tahir. "I'll have a fixed salary. My friends there really appreciate me."

"I'm on your side," said Ismail Qadri.

"Sometimes parents show us that they need to be raised all over again," added Hamada.

"Your father is not like mine," Tahir told him. "His character is more flexible."

"Their scorn drives me onward," said Hamada, annoyed.

Tahir joined *Intellect Magazine*. Meanwhile, his relationship with Raifa not only developed and grew stronger, it became known around the neighborhood, for there were no secrets in Abbasiya.

"There's no excuse for delay," he said to us one day. "I have to do what Sadiq Safwan did."

"The pasha hasn't caught his breath yet," Sadiq whispered.

"There's no avoiding the inevitable," said Tahir with contempt.

The opinions clashed at Qushtumur. Hamada urged that the marriage be kept secret until the proper time. Ismail counseled that it be done openly, then Tahir should inform his father via a letter declaring his liberation from our society.

"No," said Tahir. "I want to face the challenges on my own."

Then he continued, drowning in laughter, "Let power do with us what it will."

In these days so immersed in excitement, Ismail Qadri received the decisive blow. He led a demonstration inside the protected precincts of the university—but was arrested outside its walls. Immediately and permanently, he was expelled from the university. Our friend's plight raised a storm of pain and regret among us. His father's death had changed the course of his life, scattering his hopes, and now the holy struggle had wiped out the rest. He and his mother lived on a meager pension, and he had no choice but to contain the crisis with an immediate solution. We exchanged ideas in our sessions as Sadiq Safwan said, "You'll have to get a job with just a secondary school degree."

"We have important people who can intercede, like Yusri Pasha and Raafat Pasha," said Tahir Ubayd.

"My father is a Wafdist, and the wind is blowing against the Wafd," replied Hamada.

"Raafat Pasha is an opponent of the Wafd, but he wouldn't let us down," added Sadiq.

Sadiq had expressed a laudable idea. He went with Ismail to Raafat Pasha's mansion, where they laid out the problem for him from beginning to end.

The pasha looked at Ismail.

"So you're a Wafdist, then?" he said in rebuke.

"Like me, Pasha, sir," Sadiq broke in, smiling.

He promised to do well by them—and he was true to his promise. Ismail Qadri was hired for a clerical position at Dar al-Kutub, the national library—and so ended our friend's ambition for leadership and a career in law.

"Dar al-Kutub is right for someone who loves the life of the mind," Hamada said consolingly.

"The Wafd will return to power someday," Ismail said firmly. "But no one in the leadership knows me," he lamented. Then in a weak voice, he added, "There's nothing left for me in life but culture."

"And the prickly pear patch," Hamada said, hoping to dispel his worries.

During all this our other companions dropped away. Our councils at Qushtumur were reduced to the five of us, as we turned into landmarks of the coffeehouse. We missed not a single night through the whole of summer recess. We took up the practice of smoking the narghila, and were enraptured by its fumes.

We changed our meetings to every Thursday evening, adding the theater and the music hall to our routine. Not only did we increase the amount of wine we consumed, Hamada learned how to roll cigarettes out of hashish. Qushtumur became our most beloved place, the refuge in which we could breathe freely and exchange our feelings of friendship. Three of us—Sadiq, Ismail, and Tahir—had begun their working lives, while Hamada continued his stagnant time at university. Sadiq's situation heartened us, for he had achieved his dreams in both love and work.

How delighted he was to praise our Lord for his good fortune. Whenever he could, he would tell us, "Marriage is God's greatest blessing for His servant."

"We've now entered the sweet tribulations of the cravings!" he told us in due course.

In the days that followed, his guileless face, like clear water that never hides its innermost secrets, informed us of his urgent distress. Was this the craving, do you think?

"Her ravenous love has stopped very suddenly!"

He frankly unburdened himself of his main worry when he told us, "One of the men in her family explained to me that this condition is fleeting and temporary, and there is no cause for concern."

"We are people who have no experience in this," Hamada then said. "You'll have to make yourself happy or make yourself sad."

And so Tahir took our hearts by storm with his tale.

One night he came to us, his face drawn, and said, "The battle has begun!"

He told us matter-of-factly what had happened, and we gathered around him sympathetically.

"I've declared war!" he exclaimed.

There was nothing left between him and his parents but silence. Even his two sisters, who had married diplomats, each sent him a letter urging him to satisfy his father.

His real crisis was the clash between his love, his parents, and his eagerness for complete independence. He could not bear delay nor accept to run away. So he sought his parents out on the balcony overlooking the garden.

"I'm thinking seriously about getting married," he announced.

Contrary to what he expected, they did not respond. The most he could get out of them was the pasha asking with a preoccupied air, "Have you found a respectable girl that would do for a young man in your position?"

45

"I have found her—and she definitely will do," Tahir said calmly.

Freed from his froideur, the pasha asked, intensely perturbed, "Is it true what I have heard, that I disdained to believe?"

"What are you saying?" the hanem queried him, seething.

"I don't know what you've heard," Tahir replied, "but she is Raifa Hamza."

"The girl who is a nurse! The girl with the reputation . . ." blurted his father.

"Papa, please," said Tahir, as he stood up.

"There must be an unknown power that wants to take revenge on me by ruining my good name," swore the pasha.

"What a disaster, Tahir!" muttered his mother.

Meanwhile, the father kept on saying, "I'm warning you, I'm warning you not to bring her anywhere near this house!"

"To hear is to obey," said Tahir.

We followed him, very much moved, as he flashed a meaningless smile. "So I picked up my things and left."

"Will they give you up without a fight?" Sadiq wondered.

"I'm living for the time being in a summer house in the al-Halawani palace," he answered sarcastically.

"And after that?"

"I've agreed with Raifa that I will live for a while in their apartment after the signing of the wedding contract."

What a long trip the lover has made from a palatial home to a cramped, squalid apartment, part of which overlooks the ancient tombs! Our friend seemed to us like an adventurer who cared not at all what he came across. He chose his life with a peculiar boldness, and cut what bound him to his majestic family with a mad daring. Our talk revolved around the steps needed to carry things out: finally all agreed that he should perform the marriage ceremony at the house of Sadiq Safwan— then we would celebrate the wedding at the Families' Casino in Dahir. In truth, we could have celebrated at any place.

A room was emptied in Raifa's apartment, and it was furnished anew from a furniture dealer on al-Sharfa Street. In addition to Raifa's

mother's bedroom, the third room was made into a little living and dining room. We were having mild fall weather, so we gathered at a special
table for dinner and drinks. Raifa seemed serenely happy, but her mother
did not attend the party due to her age or perhaps poor planning. We
ate, drank, and laughed aloud. Afterward we took taxis to the bride's
apartment block.

Tahir and Raifa were both twenty years old, though Ismail surmised
that she was older. As we returned to our homes, our conversation
jumped from topic to topic.

"Our lives are but a game at the hand of Fate," said Sadiq. "So let's
bid him a happy departure."

"I admire his courage," declared Hamada. "He's a most unusual
person."

"I hope he never repents for it," added Ismail Qadri.

"Will he be able to endure his new life when he is the son of wealth
and luxury?" wondered Sadiq.

"This is like an adventure in the movies," laughed Hamada.

In any case, Tahir had now joined the Party of Stability and Happiness. By way of both Sadiq and Tahir, we learned about true,
right-guided love, like the kind we saw sometimes in the cinema, or
depicted by al-Manfaluti. As a result, they became our two productive
members—one a merchant, the other a poet. And soon, they would both
become fathers. That was better than fruitlessly roaming the sea of culture, north and south, or continuing to dissect Egyptian politics without
gainful employment.

We never imagined that Ismail Qadri would wind up a petty bureaucrat.
"Why don't you change course toward writing?" Tahir prodded him.
"That hasn't appeared in my dreams," he answered languidly.

No, we never could visualize him succumbing to the torpor of routine.
That is, his political zeal was just as strong as it had been in the past.

Only one of us remained a question mark: that was Hamada, with
his going back and forth between ideas and schools of thought, each
never lasting more than a few days. Eventually, Tahir took to teasing him
at each meeting by asking, "Who are you today?"

The evening chatter at the corner inside Qushtumur arrived at authenticity versus modernity, dazzling with all that was new in thought and science, looking toward proper governance that would bring the benefits of independence and democracy. We followed with true and burning interest the Wafd's jihad against the dictatorship. In the stream of days, Sadiq withdrew to await the birth. Ihsan's labor, when it came, was not an easy one: it required calling in a doctor to assist the midwife. After the difficult struggle, he received from his Lord his first son, whom he named Ibrahim, the father of the prophets. And so Sadiq's joy was twofold: joy at the safe delivery, and for the return of the mother to her original nature.

"I don't like the idea of having children," Tahir remarked on the occasion.

"And Raifa?" asked Sadiq, who now had experience in this department.

"The opposite, of course," he replied.

"Great," Sadiq told him. "Sooner or later, you're going to reproduce."

"I fear that that is already happening," Tahir answered in surrender.

"That's her right, and you shouldn't regret it," retorted Sadiq in a moralizing tone.

Some of us feared Tahir's reaction after the flame of his desire had gone out. Actually, he persisted in his love, proving it was a true one. He put up with his new situation with ease and gaiety. He grew more and more enthused in his work, was more and more productive and successful in it, as if he were made for nothing else. And while, like Hamada, he was a child of privilege, he seemed to have been instinctively prepared to live like one of the common people. Even his appearance differed from that of his father and sisters, beyond the habits and behavior he had gained from being around us—in which he immersed himself to the crown of his head.

In the early days of his marriage, he wanted Raifa to quit her job and stay at home. She offered no resistance.

"I am completely ready for that," she said obligingly. Then she added, "But don't you think that will add to your burdens?"

He thought and calculated, then decided to let her stay in her position, whose salary was double his own.

"Her character is worthy of all trust," he told us with great warmth. It shocked us to our souls when people talked about her past without any basis.

The time of gloom bestowed a smile upon us when the dictatorship finally fell. Yet the period of the Wafd's rule ended in the blink of an eye, after the failure of the negotiations, lasting no longer than a fleeting glimpse of the sun on an overcast day. It was followed by Ismail Pasha Sidqi, who ushered in a bloody new era of arbitrary rule and terror. The land surged with demonstrations, giving up a great many martyrs. Ismail Qadri watched the battles in Bab al-Khalq Square from the window of his room in the National Library, amazed that Fate had made him a civil servant, as he wavered between his work and taking part in the action below.

Meanwhile, we were upset that Yusri Pasha al-Halawani was forced to stay in his palace due to illness. Then he had an operation on his prostate. Soon the pasha passed away at the French Hospital, just a short distance from his home. With him Abbasiya lost the most important personality—economically, politically, and patriotically—among all of her sons, just as the Wafd lost one of its first holy warriors. His funeral procession was huge: at its head marched the Wafd's leader, Mustafa al-Nahhas. And despite the lapse in relations that befell the now-deceased father and our friend Hamada, sadness engulfed our companion on the day of separation. He wept sincerely at the burial, like his brother, Tawfiq. Yet one thing was certain—that he felt a sense of liberation and independence, and this made him happy indeed. He left the running of his father's business to his brother, detaching his own inheritance—in the form of liquid assets and real estate—from the rest. By chance, he had attained the age of majority just weeks before his father's death. To all of us it became clear that our friend was wealthy in the full meaning of the word.

"Keep good relations with your brother to avoid headaches in future," Sadiq advised him.

"I completely agree," Hamada answered, "but I get my annual share of the factory's profits without any trouble."

"Now you have to finish your legal studies," urged Ismail Qadri.

"What's the wisdom in that?" Hamada retorted mockingly.

"At the very least, so that you don't waste the long years of hardship you've spent in your life!"

"Nonsense," said Hamada.

Without hesitation or regret, he withdrew from the College of Law, not the least bit anguished about what his parents had wished for him. Freedom called on him to fulfill the dreams in his head that had pressed him onward for a very long time. So he rented an apartment in Khan al-Khalili, furnishing it in arabesque style. Then he made himself a private club in a houseboat along Gabalaya Street in Zamalek.

"How the field of diversion widens before you!" he boasted with pleasure.

The time came to satisfy his passion for the broader life, sensually and intellectually, in his long journey freed from any commitment. Just as he disdained loyalty to any idea, he rejected any ties to work. Nor was he moved by Sadiq's and Tahir's marriages. The excitement of the weddings made us long for married life. Yet he was not stirred to give up his point of view. He rotated between Khan al-Khalili and Gabalaya Street, reading and listening to recordings. He drank a little wine and consumed hashish with ardor. Then he invariably sealed his day by sitting for at least two hours at Qushtumur.

"The goal of man in all his pursuits is to attain the life that I enjoy today," he told us plainly.

"Our friend knows what's right for him," Tahir remarked.

"Just wait: everything might be turned on its head in the end!" said Sadiq doubtfully.

Then we had Ismail Qadri, living out his life as though completely narcotized to the end, a permanently petty functionary, in a house of limited income, without a future, his brain bursting with study and contemplation. Distressing doubt, along with his humble and miserable sensual pleasures, destroyed him. Why didn't he confront the difficulties

50

with the defiance appropriate to his abilities? Why didn't he shift to writing? Why didn't he study law by correspondence? Why did he surrender to defeat? When did his great determination die? It's as though all that remained of his enjoyment of the world's goodness was the eating of delicious food with a couple of glasses of whiskey on a houseboat or in Khan al-Khalili. Yet he did not lose his brilliant intellectual awareness. And when Hamada came to him with some foreigners, seeking help in appreciating the fine arts and western music, Ismail appeared to lead in these things. Perhaps Hamada's zeal slackened at times, but not Ismail's. His interest in art, literature, and philosophy paled in comparison with his love of politics and political views. In that field he remained our primary teacher.

His democratic leanings were clear. Fervently, he told us, "There is no democracy without social justice."

In appearance, at least, he remained a minor official. He continued to borrow books and to be devoted to the Wafd. His nights were spent in Qushtumur. His intimate association with sorrow was something only glimpsed in the depths of his eyes.

Tahir Ubayd—despite his self-imposed exile—ultimately made us very happy when his poetry came to be seen as the most beautiful then being published, or at least, the most beautiful being published in the prestigious *Intellect Magazine*. We would catch sight of Raifa as she came and went, dressed in loose, flowing clothes to conceal her pregnant form. At the proper time, a daughter—Darya—was born to the poet.

Tahir became intoxicated with fatherhood as Sadiq had before him, and he asked us, "Do you know if Ubayd Pasha al-Armalawi and Insaf Hanem al-Qulali know of their granddaughter's arrival?"

In reality, our friend had cut himself off from his family forever. The pasha's scowling face offered no prospect that he would retract his feelings, while the hanem was no less haughty than him. No one believed that the hanem would cease her antagonism toward Raifa's old mother. The issue became a dream or myth woven by the tortured, rebel soul of a poet.

Hamada sometimes asked him, remembering his old love for his parents, "Do you not long sometime for Among the Mansions Street?"

51

He thought for a long time, hiding his distress in a smile.

"Leave those who leave you," he said.

Then he spoke about Darya with pride.

"Really and truly beautiful," he beamed. "She's taken the best features of both her mother and her father."

"And if God had decreed that she take her father's fatness," guffawed Sadiq, "then she'd be the Bamba Kashar of her age!"

"Sadiq is not his normal self," Hamada remarked one night. "Haven't you noticed that?"

When Sadiq came later than usual to our rendezvous, we all examined him closely. He was aware of this, but ignored it.

"There's something different about you," Hamada confronted him.

He sighed, but continued to say nothing. The rest of us exchanged questions about each other's health and well-being, until he broke his silence.

"Ihsan isn't the same," he declared.

We all woke up sharply. Family secrets seized our attention, sometimes even more intensely than dictatorial massacres or philosophical ideas.

"She's now a mother, one hundred percent," Sadiq continued.

We did not understand people who live without sex. And neither did Tahir, it seemed.

"She's wrapped up in household duties," he said. "Nothing else matters but the little one."

He looked at us soberly, then resumed, "And me? I assumed that motherhood began this way, then everything would go back to the way it was. Yet my wait was in vain."

"There's time enough for everything," said Tahir consolingly.

Sadiq sighed again.

"She was a flame, now all ashes," he mourned.

"Maybe it's her health," ventured Tahir.

"Her health couldn't be better," said Sadiq, "though perhaps she has gotten plumper than necessary. She's lost her good figure, and her eyes not only have a very calm look, but a dead one, actually. She takes care of everything, but neglects herself. A totally new picture."

"Please forgive me," stammered Tahir, "but has she . . . ?"

"She responds, when she does, as a duty, not a desire."

"Has anything happened between you?"

"Never—we're in a state of perfect tranquility," Sadiq replied. "The problem is deeper than that."

"You have to have more patience," Ismail told him.

"Once I told her, 'What's wrong, my dear? Why have you let your appearance go? You were always a blooming rose.' She uses her household work and taking care of the boy as excuses. Those apologies are feeble and unacceptable. Moreover, she's happy and content, at the peak of activity. Our house is a model in its cleanliness and food. And the boy is always wrapped in gleaming white swaddling clothes. And yet, despite all that, the mistress of the house has aged a hundred years!"

Hamada looked at Tahir Ubayd.

"And how do you view that?" he asked.

"That it's an unnatural condition."

"Should she consult a doctor?" asked Ismail Qadri.

"I hinted at that to her," said Sadiq, "but she was hurt by it, and tears welled in her eyes. She's the epitome of shyness, good manners, and obedience, and considered my insinuation an insult. I told her that relations between a husband and a wife could not be based on obligatory duty— and she insisted that it wasn't like that!"

All we could do was urge him to be patient, and hope he'd find a solution. But we recognized the extremity of his circumstances. He was a man consumed by his work, and his only consolation after a grueling day was love. Since he's insatiable about it, how could he be patient in his ordeal?

Finally he confided in us, "She's pregnant again, and I'm afraid matters will only get worse."

And so Sadiq became the least at ease among us. Ihsan brought him his second son, called Sabri, while the situation deteriorated as he had expected.

"She's an exemplary lady, and an ideal mother too—and all I am is a despairing husband."

Qushtumur became a second homeland for us. Its middle-aged owner passed away, and his son took his place. The walls resounded with our voices on the news of Sidqi's fall, the Nazis' triumph under their leader, Hitler, and the 1936 treaty of Egyptian independence. During this relatively long period we observed that Hamada Yusri al-Halawani had become especially engrossed in the building across the road. There, on the fourth floor, a young girl appeared sometimes at the window or the balcony. A girl worthy of interest. She had shown up lately, part of a family that had lived in the building for a short time. From this rather close vantage point, her round, brown face looked extremely sweet, with wide eyes and sleek hair, while a halo of respectability made it clear that she was from the upper class. Then there was more news: her father was a doctor transferred from the countryside to take up a position in the Ministry of Health. Hamada took up his position—as became obvious—by the window with the best view. He consistently came to Qushtumur early in order to delight in the sight of her by the light of day.

The season was spring. In spring and summer we moved our sessions to the little garden, which offered an unobstructed view of the opposite side of the vacant road that led to Farouq Street. Hamada had reached the age of twenty-five or a bit more, and there had not been any more love stories in his life except for the fleeting one that had miscarried in a fight. After he, to indulge his whims, had set up his two nooks, in Khan al-Khalili and Gabalaya Street, his life expanded to include casual affairs. A woman would come once or twice, and then be on her way. He took as much pleasure in moving without bond or commitment as he did in going back and forth between the schools of thought.

Now, for the first time, he devoted himself to the realm of lovers. He would send a look, then he would blush—surrendering his arrogance, fast in the grip of longing and desire.

"None of that surprises me," Sadiq told him, forgetting his own sadness.

Hamada did not deny the accusation, yielding to the fact of his enchantment.

54

"By the grace of God!" exclaimed Tahir Ubayd. "We're longing for weddings and beautiful nights!"

When he sent his messages through the air and they were answered by those big, wide eyes, we were witnesses to the event.

"You've got to make a move," Ismail Qadri urged.

We loved love, and we welcomed its breezes; their distraction lightened the tension in the air charged with prophecies of war and political warnings, and cultural tempests jammed with throbbing enjoyment and violent doubts. Yet our companion frolicked and dreamed, and no movement escaped him.

"Excuse him," Ismail commented, "it's not easy for him to sell his despotic freedom and surrender his heart and his soul to never-ending chains."

But the movement advanced on the other side with outstanding courage and unsullied intent. There appeared on the balcony a pure being in an elegant robe and her familiar form on her way out to the street. She met with him an expressive look that would brook no hesitation from that point onward.

"Are we really in?" asked Tahir.

"Does she go out by herself?" wondered Sadiq.

"That was a frank invitation to which one must somehow respond," Tahir resumed. "Feel the pulse for a sign."

Hamada buttoned his jacket like one getting ready to stand up. Then she smiled radiantly.

"Put your faith in God," Ismail said to him.

The intensity of his tension kept him from smiling.

The girl disappeared from the balcony, and he left the garden impetuously. Our gaze followed him until he disappeared.

"That was an invitation to a decisive encounter," said Sadiq. "Hamada will be married before the year's end."

The next day he joined us late. He looked at us with his old, calm face, free of emotional swings and the heat of hope. We collected our thoughts and asked him sympathetically, "Shall we congratulate you?"

A cold laugh escaped him.

"Forget the whole thing," he advised.

But curiosity left us no choice.

"Yesterday I waited by the tram stop," he told us with annoyance. "Until that moment I was completely in love—just as Sadiq and Tahir were."

"And then?"

"I saw her with her mother walking toward the stop," he said. "I imagined what would happen: we would go into the first class compartment, get acquainted with each other, and sit together afterward in an appropriate place to lay out the first steps. And yes, there was only one step remaining between myself and the end—one step to take us from one state to another, from one world to another, from one philosophy to another. And in no time I found myself in a limbo that stood between my long-held dream of absolute freedom, and a tempting, transient emotion luring me to slavery. I felt horribly torn. The girl was lovely, gazing at me with welcoming eyes. And behind her was her mother, granting us the purity of legitimacy. The tram pulled up and stopped, and her mother climbed into it, then she got in while smiling at me. All I had to do was to get in and it would all be over. But I was nailed where I stood, and looked far away, avoiding her eyes. The tram moved, and I lingered in my place. I sighed deeply, savoring my survival, my limbs shivering with extreme embarrassment."

Confusion engulfed us for a moment, then we exploded with laughter.

"May God disappoint you, O distant one!"

"A very suitable girl," said another.

"You're going to regret this!"

At that, he said imploringly, "Forget the whole subject."

We fell silent out of respect for his tragedy. Perhaps we would return to the subject later. In fact, the matter was very clear on his face—this man worshiped absolute freedom, and he had the material circumstances to attain it. But how can a human being live without being committed to something? Ismail Qadri had imagined Hamada as a man incapable of loving someone truly. Yet he had loved this girl. Does love have to be like that of crazy people or even the cinematic version to be real? In this world, Hamada is like a man visiting a museum where things are shown, not sold. In the palatial mansion where he lived with his mother, in Khan al-Khalili; on the houseboat, with the professional hookers; in the library, with the hearts and minds.

"If there are too many goals, you lose the most important one," said Ismail Qadri one day.

"I admit my mistake, and say to you that Hamada will never get married," remarked Sadiq Safwan, acknowledging reality.

Hamada's brother Tawfiq got married a year after the death of their father. Just as their father had chosen their high-born mother Afifa Hanem Badr al-Din to be his bride, Tawfiq picked one of the choicest daughters of the noble families of east Abbasiya to be his. The hanem wanted to marry Hamada off too, but he thwarted her effort there, as well.

"No job, no study, no marriage—why do you live?" she asked him.

The truly evil thing was that Hamada Yusri al-Halawani's secrets had spread all over Abbasiya, and had started tongues wagging. And what was Abbasiya but a large tribe, in which no secret could hide? The people knew the story of the bewildered young girl, of his Oriental apartment in Khan al-Khalili, his gorgeous houseboat on Gabalaya Street, and he was known as the "Feeble Hashhead."

"What a loss, O sons of the notables!" mourned Afifa Hanem. "From Hamada al-Halawani to Tahir Ubayd, O heart, do not grieve!"

It was also said that our group was considered responsible for the deterioration of the sons of east Abbasiya. When this news reached us, Ismail Qadri wondered aloud with a laugh, "They're blaming a one-of-a-kind popular poet and a new Omar Khayyam?"

"The truth is that east Abbasiya is what corrupted you," joked Sadiq Safwan, "by serving you wine and hashish in Khan al-Khalili and Gabalaya. So woe to the children of good families and the scions of the aristocracy!"

But Ismail Qadri is the one who really merited the mourning. If his conditions had improved then he would have beat us all on the path to marriage, he who was known for his discipline and love of stability. Meanwhile, it seemed that the blaze of his patriotism was not extinguished, despite his intense frustration. He was the angriest and most exasperated among us over King Farouq's dispute with the Wafd—and would never forgive al-Nahhas for his impertinent resignation.

"In the old days, Ahmed Maher and Mahmoud Fahmi al-Nuqrashi used to issue death sentences against traitors," Ismail spat violently. "Now, they're the ones who deserve execution."

During this time, Sadiq's father, Safwan Effendi al-Nadi, passed away. He was the father we were most attached to sentimentally due to his famous moustache, and was buried the day that al-Nahhas quit as prime minister.

"I was absorbed in work at my shop when my father, unusually, came to visit me," recounted Sadiq. "He told me that he'd like to sit with me for a while before going off to Abduh's café in Farouq Square. I welcomed him with all love and respect. Praise God, I never stopped going to our old house on Between the Gardens Street every Friday, nor did I shirk my duty in taking care of him after he retired. I saw that he looked worryingly frail and I was seriously alarmed for him. He asked me about Ibrahim, Sabri, and Ihsan. I urged him to take care of his health, and he smiled and said to me that my grandfather had been frailer than him, but had lived into his eighties. Then he left, wishing me and my family a long life. I kissed his hand and walked with him up to the corner of Abu Khoda—and you know what happened after that."

Indeed we did, for he died when his heart stopped as he played dominos in Abduh's café. The news came to us in Qushtumur. We all rose with Sadiq and did not leave him until the man was committed to the earth. Sadiq was stricken deeply by his father's death. He prayed over his body inside the crypt, and at the condolence tent that evening we listened to Shaykh al-Sha'sha'i chant verses from the Qur'an. All the while, in our corner within Qushtumur, the talk of politics and al-Nahhas's resignation continued without cease.

Qushtumur the coffeehouse saw us take leave of our youth and our first steps into manhood. We spent our lives between work, culture, and evening conversation. Our political lives ran between hope and misfortune. It was as though we were destined to face rough, deeply rooted challenges while bound in their chains and suffering from their compulsion. Meanwhile, far from that, there were those among us who enjoyed all the pleasures available, like Hamada; or those whose foothold in the world was secured in the world by money, such as Sadiq; while others of us were waiting for worldly success. Our evenings were sometimes tinged with a new kind of discussion on the new generation: on Ibrahim and Sabri, Sadiq's sons, and Darya, Tahir's daughter. Ibrahim was now nine years old and in the primary level at the Husseiniya School for Boys. Darya was now eight, a primary pupil in the Abbasiya School for Girls. Sabri, aged seven, was getting ready to enroll in elementary school. Sometimes we asked, how do you treat your children?

"Vigilance without toughness," said Sadiq. "Exceptions can be made as well. Sometimes their boldness and lack of fear of me is terrifying—but isn't that preferable?"

"I am smitten with Darya," Tahir confessed to us, "by her beauty and her charm. I can never raise my hand to her in anger—I interpose myself between her and her mother sometimes. Raifa is much harsher in comparison with me. And there's nothing wrong with that."

We got to know the children on their school vacations, when they accompanied their parents to Qushtumur, decked out in their new clothes.

The earth's atmosphere became clouded with gloom. The human drama stretched in its course from critical development to tension, until the German armies annihilated Poland, while England and France lost no time in declaring war on Germany.

"This is the Second World War," pronounced Ismail Qadri.

"But Italy hasn't declared war!" ventured Hamada, hoping to pluck reassurance from the air.

In any case, none of us doubted that it would be declared either today or tomorrow, and that Egypt would become a battleground between the Allies and the Axis. The government took action to face the unknown, broadcasting useful information about the air raids, and turned its attention to the obligatory advisories. It painted the street lights blue, enveloping our nights in an unfamiliar blackness. We even began to dig shelters in various districts.

The wheel of our lives did not stop turning, as the news excited and awakened us.

Hamada al-Halawani's life continued between the palace, the house-boat, and Khan al-Khalili, while he added the Allies and the Axis to his vacillation between schools of thought. For a little while he'd be with the Axis, expounding on Nazism and its racist philosophy, tracing its roots back to the origins of the Aryan race. On another night he would be with the Allies, declaring his allegiance to democracy, infatuated with its historical riches and what it had given to humanity, with its principles of liberty, equality, and fraternity. He bought a Ford car of the latest model to protect himself against the oppressor and the Allied soldiers who swarmed in the streets.

"Whiskey's getting scarce," complained Hamada. "And hashish is more expensive. And, on the whole, women prefer soldiers to civilians. So what advantage do we still have as a non-combatant country?"

"War will break out in our territory," answered Ismail. "Whenever death approaches, the pleasure of life explodes," he added, laughing.

As he was invited a number of times to write songs for films, the material conditions of Tahir Ubayd's life improved. Stricken with pneumonia, his mother-in-law passed into the mercy of God. He renovated the furnishings of his two apartments by making one of them a place for living and dining, and the other into a library.

"If you visited the villa at Among the Mansions Street and took Darya with you, she would break into the hearts that are closed against you."

"I fear that Darya would not be welcomed as warmly as she should be," said Tahir sympathetically, "and that would turn my heart against my parents, whom I still love."

"But grandchildren have an irresistible magic. . . ."

"You don't know my parents the way I do," Tahir retorted with a laugh.

At this time, Raifa left her job, contenting herself with just being mistress of the house. Yet she remained skilled at, and insistent on, keeping her lithe figure. Motivated by her love for and pride in her husband, she strove to match the physique of the women seen in newspapers and magazines.

As for Sadiq Safwan, he had a story whose secrets did not emerge until its season had passed. He always seemed to us to be a glorious, highly attractive man. And especially to his customers, to whom he seemed pure sweetness, both in character and appearance. True, his problem with Ihsan had become chronic with the passage of time, and he tried to adapt to it while hiding his worry and concern. Yet one night he chose to reveal what he had concealed.

"War is evil, no question about that," Sadiq told us. "But it's not without good, as well."

We were all shocked by what he said.

"Are you philosophizing about the end of the world?" Tahir asked, teasingly.

The tale began on the day that Hitler took power in Germany. During one of his visits to Raafat Pasha al-Zayn, his host told him, "War is coming, you can be sure."

"Our Lord is over all," Sadiq answered.

"You must prepare for war, the way the Allies are," the pasha counseled him.

"Me, Pasha?" Sadiq asked in astonishment.

"The needle that you sell today for a millieme will disappear, and you'll find those who would buy it for five piasters: have you thought of that?" said the pasha. "Business is not buying and selling, but also thought and planning."

Sadiq looked at his relative, the bigger trader, with admiration—and confusion.

"Hoard every imported commodity," the pasha advised him. "Shaving kits, pens, candy—everything. Buy dirt to sell it as gold."

This was his story. We stared at him in wonder as he resumed, "I set aside a room in my apartment as a storeroom. The necessities of life that were bought very cheap were sold very dear. . . ."

"That truly would be a fortune!" laughed Tahir.

"Praise be to God, Lord of the Worlds!" Sadiq exclaimed delightedly.

Money began to rain down on Sadiq, while al-Zayn Pasha occupied the second place in his heart, after God. He bought new furniture for his apartment. He was dutiful to his mother in her old age, looking after her and giving more than what she needed in food and clothes. At the least sign of complaint, he would accompany her to see doctors downtown, better than those in the district. Yet none of this eased his anguish over his conjugal life.

"Like you, I could be excused in looking for a woman," he said to Hamada al-Halawani.

"No desire is forbidden to me," Hamada said firmly.

And while he was in this state Layla Hassan came to him to buy some school supplies. Full figured and brown skinned, exciting—with smoldering eyes—and decorously dressed, she aroused his instincts and his desire. He was not one to hide what was inside him, and so he let it show. During her surprise attack he was preoccupied the whole time, not dreaming he would see her again. Yet she came back after a few days to do more business. He rejoiced over her in a way that wrenched him out of his quotidian world, and he asked her, "You aren't from Abbasiya, I believe?"

"Are you the neighborhood warden?" she flirtatiously replied.

"I know everyone equally well—in the shop or on the street."

"We're newcomers here," she said. "We live in Uncle Khalil's apartment building near the school where I work."

"Your acquaintance honors us," he said, transported with delight.

"Abbasiya is dangerous because of the British barracks here," she remarked.

"God is our protector," he answered.

He felt that he had met with an accepting response. As he told us the story, we mused on the matter for a long time—though Hamada was the boldest among us.

"Your circumstances are bad," he told Sadiq. "You'd be excused if you married a second time."

"But Ihsan has a place of her own—Layla wouldn't have one," he said, without concealing his happiness.

"Support Ihsan, with all love and honor, with her two sons," Hamada told him. "She would understand, appreciate, and excuse it."

Eventually Layla came to him with a woman in her sixties, who announced that she was her mother.

"Congratulations," he told the mother, seeking to draw her into conversation. "They're soon going to build a shelter in your building."

"Yes," she replied with a laugh, "and in any case, if you don't look at the barracks, then Abbasiya is a beautiful district."

"Abbasiya is blessed to have the most beautiful girl living in it," he said, trying a bit of courtship.

The woman grinned guilelessly. Layla began to smile too—and the whole affair ended well.

Sadiq regaled us with what happened as his face beamed with joy. We did not doubt that he had fallen in love anew. He was a good young man: it was unthinkable that he would know a woman except through marriage. We were extremely glad that he did not flee from matrimony. The people experienced in such matters were charged with investigating the new family in Uncle Khalil's building. The information that came to us said that the young lady was Layla Hassan, thirty years of age—about the same as Sadiq—and a teacher in the Abbasiya Primary School. Her mother, Aisha, was a widow with a small pension. A family in its circumstances perhaps would not have consented to a marriage with a small goods dealer if it weren't for his fine reputation, his affluence, and his good looks—in addition to his having a university degree.

He continued to pursue his dream to its end, so we watched the new building being finished on the opposite side of the street from his shop. Entrusting himself to God, he decided to reserve an apartment for the new bride in it, should his plan succeed—and he achieved his wish.

With the war, a change fell over our quarter that brought neither joy nor pleasure. A long new road sliced between Abbasiya Street and Queen Nazli Street, tearing across the field that had provided us with the beauty of the countryside in the midst of the urban landscape. When Uncle Ibrahim passed on, the sound of the waterwheel went silent, while the lush, refreshing greenery, the sweet, strong aromas, and the clear air disappeared with it. On either side of the road, their place was taken by arid wastelands which were quickly used to sell castoff items to the British Army from cars full of rags and mounds of rubber, mechanical tools, and second-hand blankets. All we heard was the din of construction, the ruckus of the sellers, and the quarrels of the hagglers, and all we saw was the dust kicked up by the heavy trucks. The main street lost its quiet as dozens of lorries and double the number of trams rolled over its surface packed with laborers who worked to supply the British. The soldiers were spread everywhere, even in the local coffeehouses. Meanwhile, a number of mansions in east Abbasiya that overlooked the main street were sold, their places taken by tall apartment towers. The skyline started to change to that of a new quarter, jammed with people and shops, enfolding the old district with its few palaces, small, elegant houses, and its scant inhabitants who were bound to each other like the members of one great family.

As all this went on, shortly before Sadiq's second marriage and during it, our friend rushed to announce a leap forward that expanded his riches. In the big building that was being completed in front of him, he rented some large rooms on its ground floor, turning them into one large, beautifully decorated shop. He then moved into it— and was no longer merely the sole small goods dealer in Abbasiya, but also the only one whose store was similar in its appearance and displays to the shops downtown. He engraved the name, 'al-Nadi' in Kufic script on a huge sign over its entrance, that was illuminated at night by electric lights. Behind the counter sat a young man that he had hired, called Rushdi Kamil.

With his customary benevolence, Sadiq told us, "My dream is being realized, thanks first to God, and second, to al-Zayn Pasha."

"And Hitler, third!" Tahir teased him.

Sadiq set about achieving what he had resolved to do. Yet perhaps Tahir was the only one to voice anything resembling opposition.

"I believe that one wife is enough for any man if he truly wants to keep his peace of mind," he asserted.

"Ihsan is understanding," retorted Sadiq.

"Women think with their hearts," answered Tahir.

Sadiq told his mother frankly about his problem and she prayed he would overcome it. But he met grief in being open with Ihsan, until he wished that she was not such a model of goodness, and obedience and activeness, despite her gradually growing obesity. Of course, he did not confront her until he had assured himself of the attitude of Layla and her mother. Moreover, Aisha would not bless his desire to marry her daughter until he had convinced her that he had only proposed the engagement because of the illness of his first wife, whom he pledged to keep no matter what. With that, his new mother-in-law said to him, "May God bless you, for we would not like it to be said that we snatch husbands from their wives!" In general, Sadiq was pleased, even though he wished that she was younger than him by a few years. He was annoyed by some other things, particularly that she had been engaged to another man, which broke up before marriage. He interpreted this as being due to the poverty of the man's family and their inability to provide for the bride appropriately. His mother, Zahrana, had also informed him that she had no confidence in women who worked outside the home. However, Zubayda Hanem, wife of al-Zayn Pasha, had made fun of these empty ideas, saying that girls from good families today took jobs like men and that there was nothing wrong with that.

When he was alone with Ihsan he finally explained to her how he felt frustrated in a way that he never had before.

"Ihsan," he said, "God knows that you are the dearest creature in my life."

Strangely, she fixed him with an anxious stare as if her heart had guessed what he intended to say.

"I have no patience left and no other recourse," he declared. "It would be best for both of us if I took another wife."

He expected her to be angry. If that happened, it would be for the first time in their not-brief time together. She glanced at him fleetingly, her expression turning furious, as though from shock and fear—then she hid her face in her hands.

"This house shall still be for you and your children," he reassured her, "and nothing will ever separate us."

But all he met was her silence, as though she meant to punish him with it.

When he returned to his apartment after finishing his evening at Qushtumur he found only the female servant, who told him that the lady had taken Ibrahim and Sabri and gone to her father's house on Abu Khoda Street. He did not wait till the morning but went straight to Abu Khoda, where he found Ibrahim Effendi al-Wali and Fatima waiting for him. What sorrow and gravity!

"Ihsan is my best daughter," Ibrahim Effendi said, "but her luck is very bad."

"She's the best of all women," answered Sadiq.

He explained his conundrum in all essential detail. Ihsan returned home, accompanied by Sadiq, the following day. As for Sadiq, he immediately set about accomplishing what he had resolved to do. We heard the news from the beginning and followed it avidly. Aisha had told him frankly that they had hardly enough money to prepare the bridal dress, so he pledged to furnish the new apartment. Layla asked that the wedding night be held the during the summer recess, while Sadiq excused himself from throwing any celebrations in recognition of his first wife's feelings.

"We have the Families' Casino in Dahir," said Tahir.

And so it happened. We and Layla got acquainted with each other. We ate a good dinner, and Hamada took them around in his car to the out-of-the-way places of Cairo, before returning them to their new nest. And so our upright religious friend's vitality found legitimate satisfaction, as he enjoyed his bride in the blacked-out nights amid the wailing of warning sirens and the roar of anti-aircraft fire.

In the depth of winter, we were surprised by the sudden return of the Wafd to power on the fourth of February with its tanks. The voices rose in Qushtumur, both from us and from the transient customers, and clashed accordingly. The people were happy at the return of the Wafd but dumbfounded by what was said about the English armor.

"Don't you see that all of our men are traitors?" Tahir quickly quipped sarcastically.

"It's very hard to accuse Mustafa al-Nahhas's person of treason," said Sadiq. "But I don't know what to say."

"Every cabinet comes by order of the British," rejoined Hamada al-Halawani. "So why would we be upset if their order matches the wish of the people?"

But for Ismail Qadri, his zeal never abated nor was he beset by doubt. Or rather, he doubted everything but the Wafd. He seemed to approach everything with a philosopher's reason, but to the Wafd he was a simple believer from the impassioned masses.

"Don't complain about the Wafd," he demanded, "but all you like about the slanders against them!"

One night we were surprised by our first actual air raid. We awoke to an earthquake of bombs as the explosions on the ground, and not the flak fired in the air, made our houses tremble. Death rumbled all around us. We scurried into the shelters without heed to anything else. In one shelter huddled Ismail, his mother, Tahir, Raifa, and Darya, plus Sadiq and his bride, along with Ihsan, Ibrahim, Sabri, and Zahrana. Terror dug its trenches into the surface of our faces. Death appeared before us in all its closeness, tumult, and violence. The women called out, and the little ones screamed as the men clustered in silence. The raid did not last more than five minutes, or maybe less, but we were like a diver unable to breathe underwater.

At the first breath we took in limpness and exhaustion, Tahir said, his voice quavering, "Are we fated to live in tents?"

"With my return to reality, and to awareness," said Sadiq, "I found myself moving between Layla and Ihsan. Both of them were wearing nightgowns and had wrapped themselves in robes, their hair unkempt and their faces haggard. At the time, Layla looked gorgeous while Ihsan's beauty had dissolved in a vat of greasy fat."

Sadiq emerged from the terror of the raid to find himself torn in confusion between the members of his two, mutually estranged families. He went and came and came and went, while Ibrahim and Sabri clung to him, seeing the embarrassment and confusion in his own haggard face. His predicament ended only with the all-clear siren that sounded in the last part of the night to summon people back to their lives once again. Sadiq then divided his time between his two families, spending two days in Layla's apartment, then two days in Ihsan's. He had to wait a long time before his domestic life was free of tension and jealousy.

In the war the balanced tipped toward the Allies; the air raids began to wane, and, as usual, the Wafd resigned, while our lives at Qushtumur settled between ease and distress. The younger generation—Ibrahim, Sabri, and Darya—grew into puberty and adolescence. Sadiq and Tahir proudly extolled their children's academic achievement and their passionate love for culture. And yet . . .

"They witness the life of politics with all its rottenness. They have no loyalty to any of the parties."

"They have new groupings, like the Muslim Brotherhood, the Marxists, and Young Egypt."

"They are insolent and their sarcasm is bitter."

It became clear to us that Sadiq was on a mission to turn his two sons into businessmen. Tahir, on the other hand, had left Darya to develop herself on her own in complete independence, content with watching over her and guiding her as needed. The success of the two distinct friends affirmed their wealth and technical ability. Even Ismail won promotion to the seventh grade in the civil service when the Wafd was in power, although he had saved a surprise for us, which—when it was revealed—seemed a miracle of strangeness

One night Hamada al-Halawani motioned to him, laughing, "From my car, on Gabalaya Street, I saw this old fox effendi and a woman as they whispered in each other's ears!"

All eyes fixed on Ismail, accusation mixed with curiosity on our faces.

"One has to manage after the prickly pear patch was removed," he muttered.

"I'll bet he filches the antique Qur'ans in the National Library and sells them," joked Hamada.

"Do you live a secret life behind our backs?" asked Sadiq in a chiding tone.

"I waited until the story was finished to be able to tell it to you," confessed Ismail. "She is a widow with an old mother. They lived in the little building in front of my house on Hassan Eid Street."

"But it's not your custom to woo mature women!" cracked Tahir.

"She's the one who started it," he said in his defense.

"And what did you do?" Tahir pressed him.

"I responded!"

"After reaching the height of manhood, have you finally known love?" asked Sadiq.

"There's no room for exaggeration," said Hamada, "and every woman has her femininity."

"And what do you do when you no longer have the prickly pear patch?" asked Tahir.

"No, no—she's a respectable woman."

"And the solution?" Tahir pressed him.

"By signal we met and went to Gabalaya. She accepted with a lot of lamentation. She was a bit fat, as would be desirable, and succulently brown, the way I like. Her nose is a little flat, and her eyes large and wide. Her conversation is halting, as though she's searching for a way to express herself. I'd put her at about forty years of age."

He hesitated a moment, then continued, "I made her understand, frankly, that I am pinched for cash."

"That's good," Tahir agreed. "Maybe she'll be content with an illicit relationship until God brings her relief!"

"No, it's nothing like that. And I didn't stint in declaring my admiration for her!"

"That's a problem!" opined Tahir.

"To the contrary," Ismail remonstrated. "She confided in me that she's rich. What really matters to her are morality and sincerity."

"Be patient, and you'll win," Sadiq counseled him with pleasure.

We all rejoiced for him. We considered this expected wedding to be the least that this man—whose personality promised such magnificent outcomes—deserved.

Yet Lady Fatiha Asal, his mother, did not live long enough to see him settle down. She died very suddenly as she was speaking to him, without any sign of distress, like a lamp whose battery had stopped. Ismail had grown used to the orderly life under her wing, finding his loneliness worrying and disconcerting. The meeting between him and Tafida was repeated, and the bonds of their affection for each other grew stronger.

"It's painful that the man doesn't take part in preparing his own house," he told us one day.

"Marriage is more important than all of its rituals," replied Sadiq Safwan encouragingly.

It was known that her income was at least one hundred pounds a month, not to mention the considerable savings—the reality surpassed what we had imagined. There was no doubt that the woman loved him and sincerely wanted to marry him. Agreements were made to install a new bedroom and join together the old reception and dining room. While they were getting all this ready, Tafida's mother passed away.

"I charge you with killing her to get her out of the way," Tahir joked sardonically, "and demand to examine the body."

Everything was in place. The wedding night was postponed until after the fortieth day of mourning. It was deemed best not to throw any party and Ismail was content with abstaining from a celebration in which he was not able to invest a millieme of his own money. Ismail left the house in which he was born in order to take up residence in the lovely apartment welcoming his matrimonial life.

"I hope that God exempts us from offspring," he said.

But hardly a month had gone by when he informed us, "The woman is pregnant. My hope that she had passed the age of fertility was in vain."

Time passed, riding on the back of our necks like sand sweeping over the hills. The war came to an end as the first two atomic bombs exploded, and a new world was born. Sadiq remained one of the wealthy, but his life wasn't free from worry. Clearly he was very satisfied with respect to sex, and this point alone helped lead to acceptance and patience.

"Layla is obviously sterile," said Sadiq. "This is making her inwardly disturbed."

"Hasn't she seen a doctor?" someone asked.

"After a while we did," he said. "He confirmed what we thought— and made her sadder."

Hence Sadiq was not able to ward off most of his anxiety. He wanted to ease the matter for her so he told her it was not important. But she rebutted him sharply that he was already a father, so no wonder he wasn't concerned. And he learned that despite her exaggerated femininity, she was moody, quick to react, and sharp-tongued too.

"It's as though she's practicing the teaching profession at home, as well," said Sadiq.

Layla began to get jealous of Ihsan, imagining that he was eager to visit her house to find happiness in seeing Ibrahim and Sabri.

"The truth is that I'm trying to avoid the collision." said Sadiq, "as best I can."

We were sorry to hear this news. We marveled at the misfortune of our benevolent friend who was unable to experience any peace of mind.

"She's the kind that likes to impose her personality on everyone around her."

As the situation went on, or even grew worse, he accused her of feeling that she was superior to him in education. That truly annoyed him.

"She's educated but narrow-minded," he said. "She has no culture, and she's ignorant of everyday things. She doesn't know the difference between al-Nahhas and Sidqi. It's a delusion."

We grasped that he had chosen badly. We could see that she was confident of his desire for her and she exploited it nastily, showing poor judgment and behavior. But our friend did not despair.

"Time is liable to correct any mistakes."

He would be happy one night and gloomy the next. When his chest tightened, he would assure himself by saying:

"She'd be the best of women if she became more refined," said Sadiq. "I haven't talked to you about her extravagance. I spend a lot on her—double what I spend for the needs of the children in the other house. She has a lady who cooks for her at home, and wants to buy everything that dazzles her in the market. She loves to visit and be visited. If I ask her nicely to stay at home, she accuses me of wanting to imprison her and that I'm a man out of step with the times. I don't mind the expense, and I welcome any help that she offers to her mother. But beyond that I don't feel as though I deserve even a word of thanks."

"Do you still love her?"

"Truly I do love her," he said in surrender.

"You're a skilled and expert merchant," said Hamada Halawani, "but you're just a kind man at home. Ihsan Hanem did not appreciate your true nature because she is even kinder than you."

"Doesn't she remember what you gave her at the wedding?"

"Everything has been forgotten," Sadiq answered, "and I never think of reminding her about it."

"Women are arrogant—they are infidels," Hamada snapped sarcastically. "There is no difference in this regard between a respectable lady and a harlot."

Sadiq regarded staying in Ihsan's house as a relief from his troubles. Ihsan grew accustomed to her new life and perhaps found in it a kind of relaxation that was particularly suited to her. And if he found troubles in Ihsan's house, he would hover around Ibrahim and Sabri. As they excelled in secondary school they became more independent, venturing far away from the house. He would wonder and ponder, remembering the days when we became adolescents, and pray for their safety. He would invite them to accompany him to Friday prayers in the mosque of Sidi al-Kurdi: Sabri would comply, but Ibrahim would run away. He also wondered who would succeed him at his work, or help with it, but money did not enchant them. Nor did it gladden them that Raafat Pasha al-Zayn was their relative. Every day it became clearer to him that Ibrahim rejected everything, every party and organization, and that he withheld blame from no one. What did he want? At least to some extent, Sabri followed his father's life in religiosity, and therefore maybe a bridle could lead him away from it.

"The two boys are outstanding, so be satisfied with that and be happy," Ismail Qadri advised him.

"Praise God," he muttered.

But then another problem threatened the security of his first home: the health of Ihsan. He noticed that her plumpness continued to grow slowly and steadily without stopping. She puffed up in a way that not only could not escape the eye, but that began to make her less active. Her movements became ponderous, and sometimes when she sat down, she would be unable to rise without help from the maid. This was despite her abstaining from eating too much food.

"Layla eats twice as much as her, but hasn't lost her slimness," commented Sadiq.

Finally he thought he should take her to a doctor, who discovered that she had damage to her thyroid gland and prescribed medicine for her. But the medicine wasn't available, so she followed a punishing diet without result. Anxiety closed in on her; he shared her worries with a heart that appreciated her more than before. He could see no option but to hire a cook for her, surrendering to the will of God. In these days his financial activity expanded, and he bought the house in which he had been born, on Between the Gardens Street, and the house of Ismail Qadri on Hassan Eid Street. He tore them down to put in their place two new buildings that became the first of their kind, it was said, in west Abbasiya. They did their bit in boosting the population of Abbasiya while killing what was left of its traditional tranquility.

Hamada al-Halawani's wide-ranging life continued, and he did not hold back from launching his enjoyable discourses that were just like his wanderings between fields of knowledge, free from any commitment. And how concerned we were at the way his wealth kept him away from us. He loved to be with other people in new atmospheres and so stayed away from Abbasiya and Qushtumur, yet not missing a night at Qushtumur and the friends of his childhood. Because he was the only bachelor among us, his heart hung on the warmth of friendship and memories. He was not fated to receive any compensation from his brother Tawfiq for the mutual coldness that had prevailed between them since they were small. He was likewise upset by the gulf that grew between him and his beloved sister when he found out that her husband spoke about him with contempt, calling him a hashish addict. The only space left for his heart to practice emotion was Qushtumur and his old evening companions.

His mother, Afifa Hanem Badr al-Din, died in a sort of misadventure. His family was the first in Abbasiya to have air conditioning. On one of the dog days of summer, the hanem sat in front of the cold stream of air to dry the sweat pouring from her, and caught pneumonia. When they treated her with penicillin—the new magic drug—they discovered she was allergic to it when she quickly gave up the ghost. Hamada met the occurrence of her death in the middle of his fourth decade with a composure that did not match his old love for his mother. When his brother Tawfiq moved to Maadi and his sister Afkar to Zamalek, he found himself—on his visits to his mother—in a citadel jammed with helpers and servants. A whole week would pass and she wouldn't lift a finger. From here was born the idea of selling the palace. The instinct for possession and wealth stirred in Sadiq, but he feared to swallow the asking price: one hundred thousand pounds, his whole financial liquidity. He preferred not to buy the likes of this palace except to turn them into high rises, but such was not ordained for him now. Uncle Husayn, owner of the bakery, bought it and tore it down to put four new buildings where it stood.

This was the first mansion in east Abbasiya to be turned into buildings. These drew to east Abbasiya a new class of residents that would never have been tolerated there before except as tourists or lovers on a stroll. Hamada's wealth rose through his share of the price of the palace as well as what he inherited from his mother, which was close to fifty thousand pounds.

Money was one of his daily habits that nearly lost its magic.

"The microphone broadcasts every opinion without having one of its own," he would typically declare.

He was always and ever the reader, the listener, the observer, and the godless drinker and hashish smoker. But the hashish ruled him, as was apparent in the heaviness of his gaze, the slowness of his movements, and the intensity of his contempt.

"How lucky you are," Sadiq once said to him. "You're the happiest of all of us, and the clearest of mind."

Hamada shook his head to show he disagreed, but did not utter a word.

One night he told us, "When I wake up in the morning, I ask myself, 'what comes next?'"

"If a singer presents us with a beautiful tune," said Tahir Ubayd, "then we'd call out to him, 'Encore! Encore!'"

"Sometimes the heart does not welcome repetition," Hamada answered calmly.

"Has boredom started to provoke you?" Sadiq queried him with interest.

"Not true," he retorted, as though defending himself from an accusation. "It's only a passing condition. But a question is keeping me awake at night."

"A question?"

"Life gives and takes," he said. "But I only take."

"So long as you find he who gives and does not take," said Tahir cuttingly, "then there's no harm if you find one who takes but does not give."

"We're all heading with speed down that unknown road called life," an irked Hamada remarked.

"Then you give as you take and more," said Sadiq consolingly. "Don't forget what the smugglers, the pimps, the prostitutes, the owner of the houseboat, and the owner of the apartment in Khan al-Khalili, plus the many grocers, butchers, clothing peddlers, etc., have taken from you. There is no one who takes and does not give."

Hamada looked at Sadiq doubtfully to see if he was serious or making fun of him.

"Here you have the first white hair on the heads of our sheltered society," he replied, pointing at Sadiq's head.

Sadiq frowned. "No . . . impossible."

75

We strained our eyes until we spotted a hair that was different from the black smooth hair on his head. Sadiq scrutinized the accused spot in the mirrors on the wall, then he came back with an embarrassed smile.

"My father's hair turned white while he was still in the prime of youth!"

"Do you all remember how we met the first time in the al-Baramuni Primary School? It's as though that happened this morning!"

"Qushtumur too is getting old," Hamada lamented out of the blue. "It needs a coat of paint, the tables and chairs need to be fixed, the bathroom needs to be redone. . . . Only its humble garden is about as fresh as the one in the Families' Casino."

"Qushtumur is dearer to me than Roxie or al-Bodega," declared Ismail Qadri.

"Is it true that the human being's last quest is for happiness?" asked Hamada, again apropos of nothing.

Tahir Ubayd scored success after success in his poetic and journalistic life, rapturous over his daughter, Darya. In truth, she was beautifully attractive, svelte of form, with a rosy complexion, very wide eyes, and extremely thick chestnut hair. We often saw her coming and going to secondary school.

"She's smart—brave in her ideas," he said with boundless pride. "She excels in science and math. Her mother wants to see her become a doctor."

"I ask myself a lot, doesn't she love?" he added, smiling. "Who do you think is the boy of her dreams?"

"What would you do if you ran into her with a young man on Among the Mansions Street?" asked Hamada.

"I would act indifferently, as if I wasn't aware."

"Don't we have a duty to warn and guide our children?" wondered Sadiq Safwan.

"Her mother knows her duty completely," replied Tahir.

At this time, Tahir gathered all his poems and issued them in a collection entitled *The Lady Visitors in the Garden*. We each received a gift from him, and congratulated him from our deepest hearts.

Hamada decided to fête the occasion on his houseboat one night. He greeted each of his colleagues—the leftists in the lead—with a copy of the book. Articles appeared about it, and Tahir's image loomed out of the magazines. Many praised Raifa as a talented mistress of the house, a vigilant mother, and an intelligent, faithful, and affectionate wife, one who gave her husband every reason to be happy and at ease. No doubt she had changed more than expected: she lost weight excessively, and the traces of age were etched in her face. Yet she remained both beautiful and lithely built, and extremely active, too.

With all this, the concerns of the country outweighed our personal worries. The rivalry between the parties exploded and the political arena filled with mutual antagonisms, until Tahir said to Sadiq one day: "Consider me like your son, Ibrahim, who rejects all this mess."

In any case, one of us—to Tahir Ubayd's credit—became a celebrity. With steady strides he rose to literary stardom. True, Sadiq Safwan liked to think of himself as a public figure, being a well-known merchant who owned a great deal of property. Yet art bestows upon its creators a peculiar kind of halo. Did that not have any effect on al-Armalawi Pasha and his wife? Why did the portents of this escape them? The pasha retired, opening a clinic for medical analyses downtown. By all appearances he had forgotten his son completely. Meanwhile, Tahir, in addition to poetry and translation, began to write a weekly satirical column that gained him more readers.

Ismail Qadri became a father when Tafida gave birth to Hebatallah, or 'Gift of God,' after a difficult labor that ended in the Greek Hospital.

One night he came to us, saying, "I'm going to study law at home."

That pleased us all, for we saw it in keeping with the way he had excelled of old, now renewed with time.

"Have you gone back to your former goal?" Sadiq asked him.

"Yes," he replied. "I don't differentiate between patriotism and being preoccupied with politics."

Disturbing news rained down on the corner in Qushtumur: the murder of Ahmed Maher, the Palestine War, the assassination of Nuqrashi, the fight between Ibrahim Abd al-Hadi and the Muslim Brotherhood, the return of the Wafd to power, the burning of Cairo. Destiny had written that we would live through the anxieties, swallow the sorrows, choke back the anger, or blow it out in evening chatter, jokes, or comic anecdotes, together. The children entered university, and even Hebatallah went to kindergarten. As for us, we had reached the age of forty—that distinctive signpost with its echo of eternity. Sadiq had reached the peak of his prosperity. Hamada al-Halawani went to the extreme in treating his boredom with immoderate food, drink, and drugs, until he weighed more than Tahir, while Tahir attained a unique place in the world of letters. Ismail Qadri obtained his university degree, resigned from his job in the National Library, and worked in a Wafdist law office, though the most important family events were happening in the women's quarters or among the children.

First, in the house of Sadiq Safwan, Ihsan's illness grew increasingly grave until she was forced to stay in bed, too weak to move. Sadiq took care of her to the limit of his power, and we could never forget it when he said to us, "I've never known true happiness except with her."

As for his second wife, Layla, she continued to play her perverse games with him, spinning him between the twin poles of pleasure and pain, until he was completely torn between the desire to stay with her and the wish to be rid of her. He would say over and over that to the extent she was endowed with femininity she was also packed with the poison of violence, haughty without any basis as if she were the favorite. And when agitated her tongue would spit out the most detestable kinds of venom. He in his turn would not be silent so she taught him how to curse and not be sorry for what he said at times.

"Your luck in marriage is not like your fortune in business and finance," Hamada al-Halawani told him.

"I had a wife, and she was not just any woman," said Sadiq regretfully. "What a disaster, Ihsan!"

Layla's brain became more and more imbalanced due to her barrenness. So one day she said to him, "Secure my life for me by putting a building in my name."

78

What a catastrophe—she was thinking about what would happen after his death! She was reminding him of the ending that one should never bring up. What fury he felt! He was sure that she thought of nothing but his money. In reality, from the beginning she had cared for nothing but his wealth and all that came with it.

"God has a law about that, and I will not violate it," he answered her severely.

"Admit the fact that you only love your two boys!" she shrieked at him.

The difference between them grew into a feud, until they no longer traded even passing greetings, and all relations ceased. From then on she spent most of her time outside the home.

"This is hell," Ismail remarked ruefully.

"She needs someone to subdue her," suggested Hamada.

"She's ruined my life," sighed Sadiq. "Should I divorce her?"

A silence settled over us that none wanted to break—except Hamada.

"Actually," he counseled, "distancing yourself from someone like her would do you well."

"Has what I've done earned a punishment from God?"

He asked this in the tone of one serene in his piety and religiosity. We recalled some of his commercial practices that seem permissible in the eyes of clever merchants, though many others think of them as taking noxious advantage of the public. But we overlooked those out of loyalty to him and mercy for him.

"If you want to be happy with Layla, then you have to submit to her will unconditionally," said Ismail Qadri.

"Impossible," replied Sadiq. "Like fire, she can never be satiated."

"If that's so," said Ismail, "then you can't avoid a divorce."

He found that she would not quit demanding a building in her name.

"Layla," he finally told her with terrifying calm, "life with you is unbearable."

"That is what my bad luck brings me every day," she shouted.

"Then let each of us go our own way," he retorted.

"That is the most beautiful thing I have ever heard from you," she replied.

Sadiq divorced his second wife only days before the great Cairo fire. In doing so he paid a not-inconsiderable penalty: she gained the furniture, compensation for the divorce, and the customary maintenance as well.

"Peace of mind is more important," he said to console himself.

At the same time he realized that he had returned to his era of deprivation. Yet his life was not without glints of happiness—for Ibrahim graduated, followed by Sabri, from the Faculty of Law. Ibrahim then landed a post in the National Bank of Egypt after passing a publicly advertised exam, with a bit of effort as well from Raafat Pasha al-Zayn.

Sabri, however, was arrested in a sweep of the Muslim Brotherhood. He hadn't joined the organization, but to demonstrate his piety he had given money to build a mosque, and his name was found on the list of Brotherhood donors. He was cursed and beaten, then let go. His period of detention became a temporary stumbling block to his finding employment.

Then came the surprise that made all of us rejoice, and not just Sadiq's family alone. Ibrahim made his father happy by wanting to marry Darya, the daughter of his friend, Tahir. Sadiq was so delighted by this news that he forgot all his worries, at least for a while. At the very least the father's consent was assured.

"Darya and I are perfectly in agreement," Ibrahim informed Sadiq.

At this, Sadiq began to mutter, "You've overstepped your limits, Ibrahim."

"How is that?" he asked in shock.

Sadiq fell silent, holding all within him, as was his custom.

There came to us an evening more enjoyable than any we'd had in recent days. Sadiq looked at Tahir Ubayd with smiling eyes and said, "Poet, sir, your obedient servant asks to be allowed to approach you."

This moved us all, reminding us of the days passing by. Yet they had done so with the maximum of companionship, and the minimum of sadness.

"The honor is mine, Sadiq, master," said Tahir, laughing loudly. "I'd been expecting this request for some time, but you were the last to know."

A collective guffaw arose from us, capped by the gurgling of our narghilas.

Darya was an outstanding daughter. Tahir had imbued her with the love of drawing, so she entered the Faculty of Fine Arts, despite her excellence in science and mathematics and the objections of her mother. When she completed her studies, her father had her hired at *Intellect Magazine*. She was like him in rejecting the prevailing reality with a drift toward the left. But her passion for art towered over everything else.

"You're entitled to revel in your joys amid your sorrows, good man," said Hamada. "And you too should get married—the celibate's life is not for the likes of you."

"But first I have to make sure that Sabri is alright," replied Sadiq.

Sabri was starting to get his breath back after the cruel catastrophe of his arrest. When the doors to employment shut in his face, Ismail Qadri suggested to his father that he should work in his lawyer's office with him. But Sadiq did better for his son by preparing him to take over his successful trade, so that it would not be liquidated in the event of his death or retirement. Sabri decided to try himself out in the new undertaking, so his father opened a shop for him at the end of Ashara Street where it overlooked Abbasiya Square.

Then Sadiq celebrated the wedding of Ibrahim and Darya after giving them an apartment in his new building on Hassan Eid Street, right in front of Ismail Qadri's house. Tahir rented another apartment in the same building for himself and Raifa, filling it with new furniture as befit their new condition.

During this lengthy period, Hamada al-Halawani was exposed to a hidden stream of calamities flowing from worry. This heavy-set hashish smoker suffered a novel conundrum, beyond his sense of ennui and confusion.

"No matter how many kinds of ease I have," he said to us one night, "I grow annoyed with life sometimes, to the point of disgust."

We all frowned, not speaking for a long time. Finally, Sadiq broke the silence in a preaching sort of tone, "You're the only one of us who doesn't work for a living."

81

"Spare me those lectures you've learned by heart," Hamada burst in rudely. "It's a fantastic life. But it needs some bold solutions."

"Channel your excess energy into some new activity," Tahir advised him. "What do you think about traveling?"

Painful as it was for us to lose him for a while, the treatment was the right one. Hamada decided to make several different kinds of trips, beginning inside Egypt, spending his summer between various places on the North Coast. In winter he visited Luxor and Aswan. When he came back his condition had improved, though that didn't last very long.

"Go and travel abroad," Ismail Qadri urged him.

This suggestion cheered him up, and he made up his mind to carry it out. But history was preparing a new journey for the life of Egypt, forcing the man to modify his plans accordingly.

Tahir Ubayd shone as an artist, and fatherhood gladdened him to the utmost. Yet as a husband he filled us with doubt. Raifa turned forty or a bit more, yet age did not possess any one of us as it did her. Some of us concluded that she had been older than we had guessed on her wedding day. She grew extremely thin, stripping her of all bodily signs of femininity. The bones of her face stood out starkly, giving her a haggard look, changing her appearance completely. Yes, at least the old love remained on outward display, for Tahir appeared to be as amused, relaxed, and sarcastic as ever. And we wondered, what was the situation with his lady colleagues and female fans? In any case, his loyalty was the source of his high morals, which took precedence over satisfying his lusts.

Around this time, Tahir learned that his father was confined to his villa on Among the Mansions Street with a serious infection of the bladder, the signs of age showing on his body. He made for the villa, returning to it as a middle-aged man after leaving it as a youth in the springtime of life. His appearance was a complete shock: Insaf Hanem greeted Tahir with warmth and kisses, and led him to the pasha's bedchamber without first taking permission. The man peered at him for a long time with very weak eyes, then drew out his emaciated hand from under the coverlet, and they shook hands for quite a while until the tears flowed from Tahir's eyes.

"Take courage, Papa," he said gently. "I want to congratulate you on your good health the next time."

The pasha thanked him with a feeble voice, and asked, "How is your family?"

"They'd like to greet you in person."

"And I would like to see them," he answered, his voice but a whisper.

The family's visit occurred with the scent of extinction in the air. The pasha, stretched out on his bed, was passing through the final chapter of his towering life. Worry had turned the hanem's hair white, while the fluid of vitality had drained from her face. Raifa, Darya, and Ibrahim came with Tahir: Darya's liveliness and beauty sparked an uprising against the atmosphere of gloom. The hanem took her to her breast with love, while the pasha let her hand linger long in his. They tarried in the villa until they had lunch. And after some days, al-Armalawi Pasha passed away. The newspapers eulogized him as he deserved, and Abbasiya gave him a spectacular funeral. Insaf Hanem al-Qulali invited her son, his wife, and her granddaughter and her husband together to the villa. The pasha did not leave any real estate behind except the villa, plus a respectable amount of stocks and bonds and a few liquid assets, dividing his legacy between the hanem, Tahir, Tahiya, and Hiyam. Our friend Sadiq Safwan came to own two palaces—those of al-Zayn and al-Armalawi—which he alternated between from time to time. This pleased him a way that he did not bother to hide.

Ismail Qadri secured an unusually large compensation in the law office, while his mentor introduced him to the flower of the Wafd's elite. He stood out due to his well-rounded education, and held a respected place in people's hearts, attending a great many literary salons in Muslim and Christian youth associations, where he took part in numerous discussions. A brilliant future was predicted for him: we didn't doubt that, sooner or later, he would obtain his goal.

"Watch out," his patron told him in 1950, "you are going to be one of the nominees in the general election this year!"

When the 1936 Treaty with Britain was abrogated, we scaled the heights of victory. After the burning of Cairo, we tumbled into the abyss.

The momentous events kept coming one after the other, as though directed by an idiot or a madman.

"This isn't a state, but a comic circus," declared Tahir Ubayd.

We were all in a depressed state of mind, full of bitterness, sarcasm, and loathing. July 23, 1952 appeared to us like a brilliant dawn. We were overcome by a tumultuous awakening, as everything flowed like a dream. The king departed and official titles were abolished. The poor and destitute arose from the dregs and returned to the throne, as all that had been impossible became the possible. There was nothing left for us to talk about but the Blessed Movement, as the coup's supporters called it, in our familiar corner of Qushtumur.

Sadiq hurried off to his aged relative, al-Zayn Pasha (now Mr. Raafat al-Zayn), to get news from him. He was reverting to his old Wafdism.

Still, he could only say, "Truly it is a blessed movement."

Yet his voice betrayed him, and so did his smile. The look in his eye burned with anguish and anxiety.

Hamada al-Halawani remained as he was, until one day, struck by a resolve, his zeal consumed him, as though he were one of the Free Officers himself. And if a report or a rumor reached him about someone opposing the Revolution, he would turn into an implacable foe.

"What are they but agents for the Americans!" he would fume.

Ismail Qadri's mind welcomed the movement's deeds, but his heart repudiated their authors. He never disguised his Wafdism at all. The rallying of the people around the movement aggrieved him. Deep within him flared a battle between his heart and his mind.

"They should have made their base in the Wafd!" he said openly.

No doubt his personal hopes were trampled beneath the feet of the crude military movement. The amazing thing was the passion of Tahir Ubayd! For the first time in our long discussions, we saw him incandescent like blazing electricity, dancing and singing in full glory. He gave his heart and his mind without reservation.

"This was my dream," he said, "which I could not interpret until today!"

Then, in complete delight, he added, "Darya is with me all the way."

With this spirit his poetry began to pulse in *Intellect Magazine.*

The Revolution's train raced from station to station, achieving limitless victories, overcoming obstacles, and making challenges vanish.

Sadiq Safwan still repressed the unease that scorned to leave him. His distress increased when he visited the family of al-Zayn Pasha, for the agricultural reform had gobbled up the greatest part of Zubayda Hanem's lands, just as it stopped al-Zayn's activity in the stock market. The sole resources left to the family were the rent from the remaining land, that itself had shrunk by order of the new legislation. Even his son Mahmud resigned from the diplomatic corps and emigrated permanently to England.

"I'm not one of the big landowners, yet I do have property," said Sadiq. "Our turn has come—and don't you think the Revolution is an inescapable enemy of those who succeed?"

Ever and always he felt like one being pursued. He became confused about how to handle his mounting profits.

"I don't know what to do with my earnings," he fretted. "It would be idiotic to invest them in buildings. It would be stupid to put them in banks. And it would be insane to leave them in my house."

"Perhaps your mind is now at ease?" he said to his son Ibrahim one day.

"Have you never heard of exploiting influence?" Ibrahim shot back. "Hasn't the news about the secret services reached you? Don't you smell the stench of corruption?"

"It's as though you dream of another revolution," he sputtered in exasperation. "Isn't one enough for you?"

Sabri thought that he was a friend of the Revolution by virtue of belonging to the Muslim Brotherhood. Then the Revolution turned on the Brotherhood: he was arrested and brought to trial. Even though he was one of those found innocent, he lost his trust in everything. At an opportune moment he fled to Saudi Arabia and took a suitable job in a contracting company. He had become separated from Sadiq and Ihsan, but Sadiq took consolation in that his son was settled and working in security, far away from Egypt, which had begun to be ruled, in his view, by the law of the jungle. And despite his worry, he drew close to his bene-factor through his love, his sincerity, and his frequent visitations. Meanwhile, the former pasha had passed his eightieth year: his health deteriorated and he was confined to his room. His memory weakened, and the flame of his interest in anything shriveled—while Zubayada Hanem was shocked by the reversal of fortune.

Sadiq proposed to provide her with whatever she lacked.

"Permit me to return some of your kindness, which is not forgotten," he told her.

"You are like my son, Mahmud, whom I have lost forever," was all she could say.

Now the palaces began to disappear: in their place came apartment blocks and new residents, and for the first time in her history, the east and west of Abbasiya were equal. One night, Hamada al-Halawani wanted to lighten Sadiq's anxiety.

"Here's a verse for you," he said. "'The past is gone, and hope's away / but at least you have this hour today.' Chant this three times, without taking a breath!"

"But I will still think about those predatory jaws!" protested Sadiq.

Perhaps Hamada al-Halawani too was not without worry about those predatory jaws. He still hung on to his apartment in Khan al-Khalili, the houseboat, and his car. But he would often ask himself, "Who knows what tomorrow has hidden from us?"

Every time evil thoughts provoked him he would roll a cigarette, allowing it to take a whole day, drawing contempt and indifference from its magic.

"The Revolution has brought us such wonders as to make boredom impossible," he would quip sardonically. Or he might say, "The matter is clear as the sun: a group of poor people attacked the rich to plunder their money and to throw the people some of the crumbs."

He suffered his first blow when the nationalizations began. His factory confiscated, he lost his steady source of income. That did not shake his wider riches, but it doubled his fears while reinforcing his addiction.

"God grant you mercy, Papa," he jibed. "How very lazy you made me, and how you made my brother more driven to succeed. . . . See now who was wiser."

He fell ill with liver disease, and was treated for it. He could no longer drink alcohol, but had never been very enamored of it. At the time of the nationalization, he turned fifty years old: he informed us that he could no longer reach satisfaction with any beautiful woman. Thus he made his choices carefully to get what he wanted, according to his mood. And for the first time, his memory began to fail him at times.

"Death starts with one's memory," he mourned. "The death of memory is the cruelest form of death, for in its grip you live your demise while still alive."

No doubt that the clouds of tragedy spread their wings over him when he went to see his brother and the husband of his sister Afkar, who had been among the biggest owners of agricultural land. And he was equally disturbed when his father's party, the Wafd—and its heroes who towered over eternity with pride—were turned by the fanfare of propaganda from mountains into heaps of rubble.

"Once it bothered me that I took without giving," he said. "But now I repent of my repentance. Whatever a person does these days to reconcile himself to the acceptance of death is good. For if the calamity happens, we'd find in it a release."

Ismail Qadri was amazed at how Fate had intervened between himself and his hopes. Every time the future smiled on him, events would occur that wiped away his own smile. His work in the legal profession earned him a decent income. Nor did his objective mind fail to note what the Revolution had accomplished for the nation and the people, until he sometimes imagined he was a citizen of a great power. But his heart would not open to the Revolution or its men. Rather, he kept constant track of all its negatives, until one day he told us: "The Revolution has majestic goals, but Fate put it into the hands of brigands. I no longer take solace in Tafida, who turned sixty when I turned fifty. She would not surrender to reality or accept defeat, so she spent lavishly on her choice foods and her daily exercise, and a style of clothes incompatible with her age, and showing herself off so much that it makes you grimace.

"It's impossible to forget all her merit," he squirmed, "but from one hour to the next I want her to die!"

"Maybe you long anew for the Indian fig forest?" Hamada al-Halawani said, pulling his leg.

For the first time his attention fixed on Hebatallah, who was six years old when the Revolution arrived, and who was about to finish primary school. His growth presaged his giant frame, powerful features, and superiority in sports.

"He's one hundred percent a child of the Revolution," said Ismail, laughing, "and he's determined to bear it without grumbling. Don't try to correct anything he says, if you want to stay healthy!"

One evening he declared, without any occasion at all, "Life has one purpose, for which we were created and given breath," he said. "And the universe, too, has a purpose—but what is it?"

That night we fell into a lingering dialog about life and the goal of creation. We forgot our own worries for a while.

And among the individuals from our declining entourage, Tahir Ubayd shone like the moon in his brilliance, launching himself on the road to success like a shooting star. From the first day he was asked to take part in the editing of *Liberation Magazine*. Why? He wasn't one of the hypocrites or trustworthy cronies but his old populist feeling presaged the Revolution before it was born. And he was intelligent also in distancing himself from the parties. No sooner had a rapport developed between him and the officers controlling cultural affairs—he with his spontaneity and sincerity—than his feelings for the Revolution were confirmed. For what achievement, triumph, or stance made the heart of the movement throb more than his commensurate poetic gift for finding the most compelling image and immediately translating it into a song broadcast on the radio, and on television when that medium came?

"Won't you be able," Sadiq Safwan asked him, "with your standing among them, to keep the scourge from us once the order is decreed?"

"Neither poetry nor prose could prevent that," he joked.

"How sad and incomprehensible," said Hamada al-Halawani, "that you should be so sincere in what you say and write."

"Lovely poetry, with rubbish inside!" seconded Ismail Qadri.

"Believe me," Tahir said seriously, "Egypt has never reached such a summit in all her glorious ages past, just as she has never witnessed through the length of her history anyone like this miraculous man. The great man is he who transcends his personal losses to overtake the procession of history on its exalted path."

In the villa of the departed pasha, a friendly fight went on between him, his mother, and Ibrahim.

"Are you really awaiting another revolution?" wondered Ibrahim. "What are you but a revolutionary careerist!"

And he added, challenging Tahir and Darya together, "The scene has changed, but the actors have not."

"The Revolution is not without its opportunists," rebutted Tahir, "but it's enough that its leader is a symbol of perfection."

"Uncle, he is a dictator."

"Rather, he is a fair arbitrator."

Darya was happy, despite the passing of ten years in her marriage without a pregnancy. Her talent for drawing rose ever higher, along with her personal attractiveness.

Tahir's financial circumstances became very much more favorable, and he was given the chance to practice his natural propensity, generously or with extravagance, as he wished. He never allowed money to enslave his love.

The days flew by, raising some people up and making others sink down. Our corner in Qushtumur remained crowded with our presence, and was never free of us except for a brief period when the owner of the coffeehouse decided to renovate it, to change its flooring, coat the walls with bright white paint, and replace the old furniture with new. He took interest in the garden, planting jasmine at the base of its walls, adorning its corners with pots full of roses and carnations. He remodeled the rest room and bought a new set of water pipes, too. And he added two new units: one for serving ice cream, and the other—an oven—to prepare kofta.

As ever, we did not vary in our meeting, in the sacred precinct of an unchanging friendship. Perhaps what aided our remaining together was that we never left Abbasiya, regardless of all reversals of fortune. The only one of us who moved away was Hamada, yet his car would bring him to us each evening—he refused to substitute another group for us.

True, Abbasiya of its earliest days, with its quiet, its greenery, and its white tram had entered the archive of time, while shops had sprung up on both sides of the old district. Now overrun with people, the streets were jammed with youths, plus cars both public and private, in a mélange of crowds and noise and clashing souls—yet none of us ever thought of abandoning it. Nor did we ever think of spending an evening anywhere but Qushtumur, while no one from our old circle of acquaintances remained. They had all either moved to other quarters, or had gone to dwell near God when their hour had come. Our feeling of closeness grew greater, as we found in our friendship the solace of being and its sweetness. Surrender to reality overcame us, as we put many of the residues of the past behind us. We were struck by a kind of pleasant lethargy and delicious reverie, until we were jolted back to consciousness by the roar of the volcano on the astounding day of June 5, 1967. First there was surprise, questioning, and wonderment, confusion and disbelief—then surprise, questioning, and wonderment, again. We swallowed a suffering reality from which there was no escape. *How? We don't know. Why? We also don't know.* Then a torrent of talk rained down, with a deluge of jokes, a limitless playground of contradictory emotions, as the utmost sadness became the wildest joy. But the germ of depression had settled into the very depths of our souls.

Perhaps Sadiq Safwan began to breathe more easily for the first time since 1952. He was embarrassed to announce his satisfaction. And maybe his satisfaction was not devoid of worry. Yet his eyes and slips of the tongue and his endless telling of jokes that spread like locusts, gave him away. Immediately he visited Raafat Pasha al-Zayn. When he found him, he understood that events had granted him respite from the blight of old age.

Murmuring, Zubayda Hanem pointed her finger toward heaven. "He is present," she sighed.

Yet, as the result of a heart attack the pasha lived but a few days after the defeat. The hanem followed him before the fortieth day of mourning had passed. Soon afterward, Sadiq's mother Zahrana died, and her funeral proceeded from the apartment to which she had moved. Sadiq converted it into a high rise. These tragedies did not render Sadiq less affected by the grander occurrences.

He no longer felt inhibited to express his feelings.

"I have been compensated—there is a divine blessing in these wars!" he cried out sarcastically.

Overall he no longer feared the insatiable jaws after the war had pulled out its fangs.

Hamada al-Halawani rotated as usual between contradictory moods. One night he'd weep loudly, lamenting the state of the homeland, enduring the utmost pain over the dignity that had been trampled in the dust. The next night he'd outdo Sadiq in his schadenfreude and mockery.

"Wasn't it said that he taught us pride and dignity!" he'd giggle. "Have your fill of pride and dignity!"

Ismail Qadri flew into a fit of high dudgeon in profound grief when Hamada debased his wounded homeland.

"One must answer a slap with a slap, at the very least," he retorted, intensely agitated.

Then he wondered aloud in anger, "How has the ruling regime not disappeared as yet? If this man were a paid agent, he could not do more than what he's already done."

Yet no one was as shocked as Tahir Ubayd. It was though he had gone mad and expired.

"If only I had died before this," he moaned in a whisper.

"What nation has not suffered disasters?" said Hamada, hoping to lighten Tahir's distress.

"But this is the disaster of disasters," Tahir said in a defeated tone.

Spurred on by his sympathy for him, Hamada answered, "So long as we're alive, there is no escape from hope."

"What hope?" he asked, doubtfully.

"The hope in our children."

"The children of the defeat?"

Then Sadiq asked Tahir, "Have you renounced your hero?"

Silent for a while, Tahir replied, "I suppose he will die now, and I will die with him."

Our desire to meet only increased, even though it was no longer for us a pure means of relief. For us there was only one weighty discussion: a sour political repast—we slept and its bitter dregs mixed with our saliva. The scarcity of laughter perhaps frightened us into contemplation and philosophizing. We spent the rest of the year, and the year that followed it, continuing in one mode as we edged closer to sixty.

"An important conversation took place in the shop today," said Sadiq Safwan one night. "Our neighbor and her daughter came to buy some things."

This excited interest in our placid souls. We speculated about the surprising—and pleasing—bit of news.

"Amouna Hamdi and her oldest daughter, Sina Ibrahim!"

Were the names not drawn from those we knew? Amouna Hamdi was a divorcée of about forty, from an acceptable background to which no one could object. Sina was a girl of about eighteen springs and of ample beauty. They lived together under the wing of the father—the daughter's grandfather—Ali Barakat, a bureaucrat of limited means, and his wife, Khadiga Allam.

"Amouna is a woman appropriate for a man of sixty," pronounced Hamada al-Halawani.

"But my eyes were fixed on Sina."

"She could be your granddaughter," said Ismail Qadri.

"Life isn't measured in years," he protested.

"The difference in age is truly great," said Tahir.

"She reminds me of Ihsan at the peak of her luster—an American apple, lively and intelligent."

"You suffered failure twice before," Ismail reminded him. "Each time bad luck was lurking behind it. This time, you're making your own choice."

"The happy ending can come from where you don't expect it," said Sadiq, beaming.

"Would the mother and her family accept a groom of sixty for a young girl of eighteen?" Tahir asked incredulously.

"Men are weighed in piasters these days, more than at any time in the past," Hamada interjected. "The girl lives in a poor home in the care of her grandfather, so our groom would be considered a stroke of good fortune."

"I imagine that the woman came to show herself and her daughter to me, so I could make the choice appropriate to me."

"And your choice is not the appropriate one," retorted Tahir.

"Know your foot before taking a step," admonished Ismail.

"How much more appropriate would it be if we directed this proverb to the hero of June 5?" mocked Sadiq. "As for me, I trust in myself. Long have I been tortured by celibacy and self-denial, and God knows my situation."

He didn't waste any time. He pursued his desire, and met with acceptance. Meanwhile, our eagerness to affirm our friend's happiness and to give the lie to our suspicions forced us to do nothing. As usual he bore all the expenses, choosing the apartment in a brand-new building in Army Square—formerly named after King Farouq—and achieved through generosity what he had missed in pleasure, to compensate for his anxiety when he had faced the predatory jaws.

"We are in an age when the impossible happening surprises no one!" exclaimed Ismail when we were alone with each other on our way back to our homes.

What he said seemed a kind of preparation for the unexpected transformation that befell the life of Hamada al-Halawani. He was not sparing in his complaints about lack of activity and boredom.

"You have an accurate picture of my life," he told them. "I'm a man who prepares carefully in an orderly manner to wait for a sleep that does not come! Every day is heavy, nothing new in it," he groaned. "Discontent is the cancer of the soul," he continued, as he looked back and forth between Tahir and Ismail.

93

"What's the point of circles of friends then?" Sadiq queried him.

"Even a stoned person can get depressed," he shrugged. "The only relief I find is in Qushtumur."

And in the flood of preparations to fête his sixtieth birthday, he came to us and said, "Men, get me married!"

We all laughed for a long time. But then he said seriously, "I mean what I say—get me married: I need a wife!"

We were thinking quietly when Sadiq piped up, "This is what I had predicted for him."

"This is nothing more than an attempt to kill boredom," added Hamada.

"You're a man who'd be considered a catch in the noblest of families," Sadiq told Hamada, whether sincerely or in flattery.

Whatever was said, he was, in fact, more infamous than the Fifth of June. What family would see him as other than that languid, dissolute hashish smoker, not to mention his advancing age? The girls of the day were not like those of earlier times, and it was rare to find another set of circumstances like those of Sina, wife of our friend Sadiq Safwan.

Every one of us searched on his behalf, and all we met was rejection, until Sadiq said to him, with his accustomed benevolence, "What about my mother-in-law? She's very acceptable, and I believe she would agree."

"I should break my fast with an onion?!" Hamada snapped dismissively.

The agitation from his repeated rejections enraged him, provoking his wounded pride.

"Professional women would be better than these virtuous maidens," he roared.

This made us all frown.

"Slow down," Sadiq insisted, "or you might find yourself in perdition."

"No one knows them as well as me," he said derisively.

Hamada struck out on his path with resolve, renting an apartment in Zamalek, furnishing it like a museum. He invited us to witness his bride at the dinner table at the Auberge. We found the bride to be a woman in the middle of her fourth decade, with a succulent body and a beautiful face. Her wedding dress did not dispel the air of debasement about her, while the glance of her heavy eyes dripped with experience and bad temper. We thought that this phony straight life did not fit with his true nature as much as his libertine life had. Had it been based on love, then we would have excused him, but we sensed it was only due to his stubbornness and pride. As for him, he affirmed for us, in Qushtumur, that she was superior to any virtuous girls, and was herself from a good family. All we could do was to wish him success and happiness.

Ismail Qadri hit sixty while working in the law office in which he achieved a notable success. Tafida had turned seventy, succumbing to age and surrendering to reality. She began to suffer from headaches, and circulatory problems in her legs. Hebatallah graduated as an engineer at the age of twenty-four. The defeat and the hero's fall broke his heart, and he fulfilled a dream that had long tempted him—and that was to move to Saudi Arabia.

Tafida was desolate, but Ismail told her, "He is not less worried than you, but perhaps he'll find some comfort in the pay."

Neither his work nor his success made Ismail forget his political grief or the defeat of his homeland. To these were added the wilting away of his wife and the emigration of his son. We noticed in this period that he tended to talk about spiritualism and the miracles of parapsychology. Certainly, he had come across them before in his cultural tourism, just as Hamada's contradictory wanderings were not free of them either. But Ismail found, in the sayings of the Sufis, a new form of magic. He hovered around it, and was intoxicated by it, seeking out its kiss like an exquisite cure for the heart.

"Admit that you've gone back to religion," said Sadiq plainly.

"Don't oversimplify things, or they will lose their meaning," he answered with displeasure.

"The nights are pregnant with miracles," proclaimed Tahir. "From the outside, there is no end to the chain of catastrophes." Ismail seemed torn between his pride and his compassion.

Tahir Ubayd felt sorry for the leader even more than the leader felt sorry for himself.

95

One night he recited to us his poem of eulogy, soaked in sorrow, bitterness, and self-satire. None of us listened to it with sympathy. The media had stopped playing his songs, for they could not be heard except in an atmosphere of victory.

One night he confessed to us, addressing his comments to Ismail especially, "My wife is in a state even worse than your wife's."

"They gave the best of what they had," answered Ismail.

"I've started to loathe her," Tahir said brutally.

"Everything is loathed in the end," replied Ismail.

Tahir declaimed a great deal of poetry overflowing with despair, sadness, and pessimism, much of it clearly influenced by the art of derision. He did not publish anything that might have harmed the wounded hero, even indirectly.

"See how he's purifying the Revolution of its negative aspects, and how he's starting to rebuild the army," Tahir said, clutching at any thread of hope.

"Sisyphus will scale the mountain once again!" Ismail mocked him.

Tahir no longer answered the taunts after his soul was shattered, his pride defeated. When the man himself left this world, his sudden exit struck Tahir a fateful blow.

"Let me repeat with the believers—and I am not one of them—that all things perish except His face," he said.

Sadiq Safwan, however, could not conceal his joy.

"This news is more exciting than a honeymoon," he exulted.

"His death is one of his most glorious deeds," deadpanned Hamada.

"He went at the right time," chimed Ismail, "leaving the deluge to whoever follows him."

Sadiq launched himself into a new confidence: "I'm optimistic about the new president," he declared.

He was deliriously happy with Sina, and felt he was king of the world. Perhaps Sina wasn't as simple as he wished, for she was not exactly like Ihsan. She had obtained her secondary certificate just before her wedding.

"I want to complete my studies!" she told him with passion.

"I didn't finish my studies beyond secondary school," he replied, disturbed, "but wanted to work instead. Do as I did, while laying the foundations for your life as a housewife."

"My dream was always to finish my studies," she said softly.

"That has no significance whatsoever," he reproved her.

"Every girl does this today," she persisted.

"And you want to follow blindly?" he sputtered.

"Never," she said, "but knowledge has a value too."

"But it's not as important as you being a wife and then soon becoming a mother."

"Some of the female students at university are married," she continued, with a stubbornness that irked him.

"Never would I allow my wife to enroll in the university and have her mixing with the students!" he said with a sharpness that overcame his love and tolerance for her.

"Don't you trust me?" she demanded insistently.

"Absolutely," he answered, "but my dignity will not permit that."

It occurred to him that she would not have consented to marry him except for the pressure from her family and her austere circumstances.

"Let it be understood," he decreed rigidly, "that I will not agree to it."

She fell silent, conquered by his command. She later attempted to convince him to let her complete her studies by correspondence outside the university, but he wasn't at ease with that either.

He recalled what happened due to his docility with Layla, and told us firmly, "Not this time. What's agreed at the start must be kept at the end."

We grasped that the lesson Layla had taught him had not been erased from his heart. It pleased us to imagine our mild-mannered friend as a lion in man's form.

"There's a demon lurking in every ruin," said Ismail Qadri.

"But I slew this demon in its bottle," he answered with assurance.

None of us approved of his approach, but we avoided bothering him with our complaints. She proved to them that she was as active a housewife as she was a beautiful woman. We understood that she had sacrificed her hopes in order not to return to the shameful corner in her grandfather's house, especially as her father did not appear in the picture at all, whether by his insignificance or by his absence. And on more than one occasion, Sadiq praised her liveliness and activity, attributing the discovery of her merit to his firmness with her.

"I wasn't able to go back and forth between her and my library," he said, "for all of her spare time is spent reading. I didn't see any harm in that, but once she said to me, 'Knowledge is more important than money itself.'

"I wasn't happy with that statement," said Sadiq. "If I hadn't been so diffident, I would have reminded her that my money has brought her things that knowledge of this world and the next could not have done.

"'The men of finance are the most important in society,' I pointed out to her. 'An awful lot of the literati are not only unable to make a wife happy, they are even unable to marry to begin with.'"

"How amazing that you have been on intimate terms with us all our lives, and that you hold such an opinion!" laughed Hamada al-Halawani.

"Women have their own language, and there's no point in talking with them except in that language," he said.

As much as we wished him every happiness, we were assailed by doubt over his success in the end. Sina produced Nuha for him from her womb. His heart was full of warmth and happiness.

Time kept passing us by, nudging us each day a step further into our seventh decade. Astoundingly, our health competed in strength with our worries. The era of the second leader was also full of its own surprises—for this was the epoch of pulpits, victory, peace, and al-Infitah, as well as the greatest degree of corruption ever recorded, both in its extent and its sordidness. We had hardly grasped the change that had befallen us then. When, as in the old days, we went out for an occasion, we'd compare what we had been with what we had become, perplexed by the transformation. This only increased our closeness and affection for each other. Qushtumur itself became one of us, just as we became one of its corners. We would exchange glances as we remembered those who had passed away, all the while knowing that our own days were coming.

"What a life!" Sadiq Safwan mused one night. "My son Ibrahim rejects those who reject the rich, while my wife doesn't give money the place it deserves. Does this not reflect her secret feelings about me?"

He was overjoyed by the victory of October, then by the peace with Israel, and by the trend toward democracy as well. But he was not without worries or cares.

Ismail Qadri tried to dispel his fears. "The marital framework is stronger than any philosophizing."

"But we're also in the age of money and millionaires," added Hamada.

"Where are we, and who are they?" asked Sadiq. "I'm just an old-fashioned fellow from the group that the present age is sweeping into poverty."

Many people spread rumors about deals and imaginary riches. And in that time, his wife's family passed away. First Ali Barakat, then her grandmother, Khadiga, and then his mother-in-law, Amouna, each departed from this world. Meanwhile, at the age of four, Nuha went to kindergarten. And he was distracted, as he distracted us as well, with a new idea.

"What do you know about lady tutors?" Sadiq asked us.

We couldn't help but smile at the blush on this face.

"This is not a joke," he scolded us.

We were sure he was serious, without a doubt.

"You have to get specialists—that's the recommendation," said Ismail.

We shared in his anxiety, which he did not express directly. And when Ihsan moved to the mercy of God, he grieved for her sincerely.

"The most perfect of women," he mourned. "If it weren't for her overwhelming illness, then I would have been destined to receive from her happiness unknown to man."

He added, "The worst kinds of exile are those that you feel in your own homeland. God curse these times. They take the people closest to us and make them our enemies. And the truth is that you, my friends, are the dearest things to me in existence."

99

Sadiq was the first of us to know sickness, as his joints were stricken with a particularly painful case of rheumatism. He consulted many doctors, became accustomed to taking medicine, and even changed his diet.

"Praise God for our faith," he said. "It's a comfort in this world and the next. Each time an intimate friend or group of friends has disturbed my serenity, a pain or trouble was drawing near. And every time something of that sort has afflicted me, I remembered God on high—savoring His welcome and surrendering my concerns to Him. How He inspires me with patience and contentment."

A good ending, or not bad one anyway, if it weren't for the bomb that Hamada al-Halawani exploded beneath our feet.

"Friends," he said, "I've come by car to tell you that I saw Sadiq's wife signaling suspiciously to a young man who lives in the building next to theirs."

We received this news like the most evil doom that weighed down upon us from the world of the Unseen. We traded looks that were not only confused, but which appealed for help—questioning insistently, and heavy with worry.

We were silent for a while until finally Tahir said, "Maybe you're mistaken, either in what you saw or in your interpretation of it?"

"I'm dead certain about what I said," replied Hamada, scowling intensely. "Think before he comes."

"The matter is very dangerous," fretted Tahir Ubayd.

"We have to take a decision," Hamada declared.

"We have to be certain," said Tahir.

"I am indeed certain," asserted Hamada.

A heavy silence prevailed upon us Hamada said, "We are obliged to inform him."

"Maybe we will destroy him," said Tahir.

"Can we keep what we know from him?"

"There's no escaping that he's going to find out, one way or another," said Ismail.

"The scandal might drive him to commit some crime," fretted Tahir.

We looked at each other again for a long time, then Hamada asked, "What would be the right outcome for all this?"

"That he knows, and it ends without dangerous complications."

"The sin cannot go on forever—it has to end," insisted Ismail.

"It's not in our power to withhold it from him," said Hamada.

"Leave it to me," said Ismail Qadri.

When Sadiq Safwan arrived, Ismail took him into the garden. We were at the end of autumn, so it was empty. An hour went by, an hour that seemed heavier than death. Then the two returned to us silently, and we took up our session. Oh the image of that noble person at the moment of defeat! We consulted on the matter until we had encompassed all his emotional reactions.

He asked for some time to consider the matter. The days passed until he came to us at the appointed hour.

"What do you suggest?" he asked us.

"Here is a solution that suits your wisdom and your piety," began Ismail Qadri. "There's no getting around a divorce, and you must keep Nuha. Nor would it do to leave the other one a prey to poverty. An agreement would be better than a court ruling. Rent an apartment for her and provide her with an income in honor of her daughter. I reiterate that this would accord with your piety."

I believe that Sadiq exerted a monumental effort to suppress his desire for punishment and revenge. And indeed he did the right thing in a way not done by anyone before: he divorced her while preserving her dignity; he kept Nuha to close the curtain on the tragedy. He returned to his loneliness, but it turned out not to be absolute this time, for near him were Nuha and her nanny. Thanks to that, to his age, and to illness, he no longer suffered from his former sense of deprivation.

A group of people came to propose that they buy his shop to turn it into a boutique, one of many that opened with al-Infitah.

"The only certain things in my life are my shop and Qushtumur," he muttered.

"If I was in your place, I would have closed the deal," admonished Hamada. "The amount is fantastic—and afterward you could relax."

"There's no one to follow me in my work," acknowledged Sadiq. "Ibrahim has his own world, and Sabri adapts himself to wherever he is. Until when will I keep working from morning until night?"

He sold his shop, freeing his time for the raising of Nuha and to calm his rheumatism, to read the Qur'an and the Hadith, and to perform the obligation of the Pilgrimage. Yet our corner in Qushtumur remained the delight of his eyes. Hamada al-Halawani too was one of those over-joyed by the October victory, and who welcomed the peace as well, but with an unshakeable serenity that resembled Buddhism. He freely admitted that his marriage had ended in fiasco while he was savoring his honeymoon. Sometimes a smile would appear in his eyes that seemed to ask, "What have I done to myself?"

The truth was that he did not experience any real change in his relations with the opposite sex, nor did he get rid of his wife due to her professional background. She remained his lover, but did not act like his wife. She was preoccupied day and night with adorning herself, and with her settled habits of drinking and smoking hashish, all the while neglecting her domestic duties, just giving orders to the house servants instead. Nor did she cease her demands for money, continuing on her mission from the first day.

He hoped for a change when she became pregnant, but the fetus died in her womb: the operation and the uproar were in vain.

"We don't talk outside of bed: I might listen but don't know what to say," he said, venting his complaints to us.

His feelings of loneliness and boredom multiplied. He tried to escape the beautiful apartment at any excuse, saying that loneliness without her would be lighter on the heart.

We expected to hear about the divorce in the very near future. Sadiq Safwan asked him, "Is she malicious?"

"She's trivial," answered Hamada. "We don't allow any opportunity for her evil to manifest itself. She's just frivolous: prostitution kills the humanity in the heart of a woman, and makes real misery possible."

"What do you want to do?" asked Sadiq in a melancholy tone.

"Divorce her, of course," he laughed.

"But the issue isn't easy," he explained after a brief pause, "and won't be resolved except after a bloody battle—scandal, disgrace, a trial, and a good fleecing. And she wouldn't hesitate to fight with me or confront me on the street."

"One day you said that professional women are preferable to amateurs," Tahir Ubayd reminded him.

"Don't remind me of what I said," answered Hamada. "She will try to get the most she can out of it."

"Buy yourself some peace of mind," Sadiq advised him.

This was what he was determined to do. It began with the call to breakfast. He was not accustomed to holding things in, so he started throwing the food around while flashing defiant, censorious looks at her.

"It's obvious that I'm not made for marital life," he bellowed.

"Did you marry me as an experiment?" she answered impudently.

"It's better that we separate, the same way we came together," he told her, softly. "I hope that you will forgive my mistake."

Her tongue poured out a stream of obscenities. He sat with patient silence, then told her that he would seek a mutually satisfying agreement with her far removed from any court. She demanded a million Egyptian pounds, preferring to settle the matter at trial. After a struggle of give and take, she was happy to get a quarter of that.

"This was a calamitous loss in an age of madness," Hamada admitted to us. "My wealth has no value today: the high cost of living eats the desert and the sown. I pay forty or fifty pounds now for what I used to buy for fifty piasters! Yet the boredom is a mercy compared to the company of that insipid tart!"

"In any case," said Ismail Qadri in consolation, "if you want to marry a true wife . . . ."

"I've repented of all that!" Hamada cut him off peevishly.

He considered his return to the life that had formerly annoyed him to be an enormous gain.

Then it happened that, most unusually, he stopped coming to Qushtumur—first for one night, then another. The friends went to his usual haunts to investigate the secret of his absence: Khan al-Khalili, the houseboat, and the apartment in Zamalek—and thus we learned the disturbing reality. That is, he was being treated in the Maadi Hospital for an attack of angina pectoris that had caught him unawares.

We rushed to the hospital in extreme panic. His brother Tawfiq and sister Afkar received us there: they brought us peace and confidence by saying that he had passed through the danger, but he was not allowed visitors for several more days. Tawfiq had become the very image of Yusri Pasha at the end of his days. Yet Afkar appeared weak and ravaged by age: her body emaciated, her face creased and crumpled by time, as though the beauty that once sat on the throne of her form had perished in an arbitrary judgment.

"How much greater the havoc that time has wrought upon her!" murmured Tahir Ubayd.

When we all visited him two days later, Hamada's joy at our presence around him overflowed on his colorless face. Then he spoke to us about his angina.

"When it comes, it's frighteningly fierce," he said, "and when it's over, and a man returns to his natural state, it is as though he had never been within an inch of death."

He recounted that he'd been by himself, as stoned as he could be. He rose to eat his supper at a late hour of the night when an electrical shock ignited in the upper part of his chest. The pain squeezed him until it seemed it would choke him—he stumbled about, screamed, and then threw himself down and rolled about on the ground. The maid contacted his brother's house: he came in the company of a doctor, then moved Hamada to the hospital.

He was released after three weeks and returned to Qushtumur, to fill the place that only he had occupied. Meanwhile, regular medicine and a strict diet had arrived at his door.

"They want to steal the last remaining taste from life," he complained. "There's also a regime for rheumatism, and by necessity, a bunch of rules as well."

"Yet life is a matter of to be or not to be," said Sadiq Safwan.

Eventually it became clear to us that he stuck to taking his medicine each day, but he ignored the diet as though it did not exist. Hamada clung to his accustomed foods with all boldness and contempt. Nor did he deny himself kif or consume less of it.

We lectured him about this, but he showered us with wisecracks in reply.

"Have you decided on suicide?" asked Tahir Ubayd.

"I've decided not to be scornful of the love of life!"

Nor did he give up on women completely. He still had them over, if only once a month.

"Doesn't age exempt you from this obligation?" Sadiq asked Hamada with a grin.

"But that isn't appropriate to my condition," he cackled.

Tahir Ubayd found himself under the rule of the second leader in a world that he hated and could not endure. He was oppressed by the thought from the first moment, regarding him as an agent for every reactionary power, both foreign and domestic. He didn't tarry before resigning as head of *Intellect Magazine*, though without leaving the staff. The bigger blow came when he was banned from writing, without any direct justification or accusation. He was furious, and so were we. Nor did he leave a trace in any of the mass media. And when the great victory came, he met it with a strange torpor, while attributing its roots to the departed hero. He was the only one of our group who worshiped the deceased during his lifetime and sanctified his memory after his death. If it weren't for our extraordinary friendship then perhaps we would have been irritated by him and taken our leave from him. Yet he remained with us, stood up against us, matching serious statement with serious statement, and jest with jest.

Tahir limited his activities at this time to publishing some poems in Arab magazines published abroad. Shortly after he became sixty years old, he had a chance encounter of a sort that had never happened to anyone in my experience. He got to know a new female editor, Anwaar Badran, when she joined *Intellect Magazine*. She clearly was one of his devoted readers: her admiration of him exceeded all his dreams. She visited him several times in Qushtumur and got to know us too. We learned that she was a literary graduate of the English language department. We found her utterly intelligent, highly cultured for her age, which had reached twenty-five years. Slender and brown-skinned, with regular features and narrow eyes, and a small, flattened nose, she was altogether alluring.

After sharply observing him, Ismail Qadri asked Tahir one night, "Do you love your pupil?"

"Yes," he answered, tersely and directly.

"Could you play in the modern way, perhaps?" said Hamada al-Halawani.

"But my feelings are serious!" he bridled.

"I thought you had loved enough by now," said Sadiq Safwan.

"Love has no laws," Tahir answered.

"And Raifa?"

"That finished a long time ago," said Tahir.

"Our group should teach a class on sex," laughed Ismail Qadri.

"Precaution cannot thwart Fate," said Tahir in surrender.

Strangely, at that time his daughter Darya became pregnant for the first time in her marriage, when she was already past forty. She had seen doctors about it, and despaired of it ever happening. Rather than wait for the arrival of his grandchild with the proper deportment, he gave himself up to love. He came to us one night drunk with joy, such as we had not seen in him for a very long time.

"We're going to get married!" he beamed.

"All we can do is congratulate you."

"And Raifa?" asked Sadiq.

He bit his lower lip as he replied.

"There was no choice but to be frank," he said. "A difficult, painful situation, but I'm used to confronting challenges. She was convinced that she would no longer possess what had been given to her. I reassured her from the first moment that she would remain in her house, as honored and as cherished as ever."

Quiet for a moment, he then resumed, "She said to me calmly, but with a shaking voice and eyes shining with tears, 'Accept my regrets, but

I have no choice in the matter.' So I told her, 'I'm convinced that I was in error.' She answered, 'There's no doubt of that: great wisdom came to you at a time when you didn't need it badly, but you lost it at the hour you needed it most—may Our Lord be with you.'"

With intense anxiety we pictured the tragic wife, now that time had turned against her, discarded like dross.

"Surely she is swallowing a kind of bitterness such as no one can imagine," said Sadiq Safwan. "I saw Ihsan in a state like hers, despite the clarity of my excuse, and its strength."

But happiness carried Tahir away, sweeping in its path his hesitant emotions. Sometimes he seemed like an innocent child, reminding us of his bygone days of untrammeled victory.

"There is nothing sound and true in our world," he said to us, by way of apology. "So why should I demand it?"

For the first time, Darya disagreed with him, denouncing his decision.

"Papa, I couldn't imagine," she reproved him.

"It's something natural that happens every day," Tahir told her, smiling.

"And Mama?" she asked with tenderness. "We just wanted fidelity— which is as beautiful as love."

He related what she had said with hidden pride. Still he persisted on his path with his well-known élan, yet told us like one seeking pardon, "Love is love—and to me its presence destroys all powers of opposition in the blink of an eye."

Then, as he searched for a new marital nest, a new problem confronted him that did not exist in our earliest days—how to find an apartment. But the solution was not too difficult, for after a not very brief effort, he found a new lair in an apartment that he got without having to pay a bonus to be given preference. He greeted his new life as though entering a world for the first time. Anwaar did not make him happy with love alone, but aroused him with her intelligence, her truthfulness, and her genuine love of culture, not to mention her profound relish for his poetry.

"She would fit right in as a member of our group," he told us.

Anwaar decided to postpone getting pregnant, which pleased Tahir greatly. Yet she lacked any political loyalty, for she did not always believe or take interest in what she heard or read. Her mind was focused on poetry and its criticism, and she tried to compose verses on occasion.

"The only political seriousness is in the religious tendency," she said when he declared his Nasserism to her.

"Is that approval?" he asked, disturbed.

"Not at all," she said. "But they're the only ones who stand on solid ground in an ocean seething with unrest and depravity."

"Does it seem to you that they have hope for their side?" he asked, his anxiety rising.

"Never," she answered, then asked him, "Why don't you emigrate? The high cost of living here is compounded every day—and you'd find splendid opportunities abroad."

"Not every chance has been destroyed here," he rallied. "There are private-sector theaters that ask me for songs and musical revues."

"How can you disdain your reputation and be content with your decline?" she wondered.

We told him frankly that it was not wise that a person think about emigration as he nears the middle of his seventh decade.

"Your acceding to the requests of the private sector could lead to higher things," said Sadiq Safwan.

In reality he responded to the inducements of the private sector under the pressure of living conditions and his duty to provide for both houses. He exercised his talent to the utmost in order to avoid falling, yet feared that his exemplary image had been compromised in the eyes of Anwaar. His profits increased but in Anwaar's eyes, an absent look appeared, warning of what lay behind it, vindicating our fears.

We expected over the course of time the rabab would play the melancholy tunes that we were used to hearing from Sadiq and Hamada. During this time Anwaar conceived by choice, but she suffered a difficult labor and the baby girl was stillborn.

"Not only that," said Tahir, "but she has decided that she will not be a poet and has given up the attempt."

In any case, her career advanced as a critic, and she still had the ability to get pregnant again and give birth to a splendidly healthy infant. Tahir was overwhelmed by the memory of his past in the shade of his present, and his worry and concern doubled. He seemed to have awoken from his reverie, realizing that he really grasped nothing in his hand but air.

"Your friend is finished!" he told us.

We looked at him questioningly.

"We have both moved into separate rooms," he said. Then in a hushed voice he added, "The relations between us are as good as they could be."

Anwaar was offered a job in an Arab magazine published in London, and expressed her desire to travel. He could find no excuse to refuse.

Perhaps Sadiq Safwan was the only one of us who told him, "This situation is not correct."

Tahir returned to Among the Mansions Street to live once again with Raifa, Darya, Ibrahim, and his new granddaughter, Nabila. He launched himself anew into the convenient field of art, a long way from Anwaar, who tortured him for a while like his missing conscience. He had retired on his pension, but the money flowed in his hands both freely and copiously, until he remarked to us sarcastically, "I've become one of the nouveaux riches of the Infitah."

Yet in his depths he was deeply, deeply sad, pursued by the feeling that he had fallen.

"What is the sweetest hope of my life?" he asked us one evening.

"That the leader will die or be killed?" suggested Hamada to him sarcastically.

"Death," answered Tahir. "I wish for death—I plead for it."

He said nothing more until we had finished our protestations, then went on, "If it weren't for Darya, or if not for Darya and Nabila, I would have committed suicide. My esteem for them, and shame for them, have prevented me from doing it."

"Your older poetry will always remain a lofty example that forgives what came later," opined Ismail Qadri.

"Is it a crime for a person to defend himself from the havoc of hunger and poverty?"

Ismail balked for a moment before continuing, "How could your recent works be lower in quality? In my view, they are as beautiful as your early work, if not more so."

As he approached his seventieth year, he was struck with a urinary disorder that was not benign. The doctors discovered malignant cells in his prostate, and prescribed an experimental treatment for him. If it wasn't successful, there was nothing for it but an operation.

He regarded the illness with manifest disdain, muttering hopefully, "Maybe this is the end."

One night as we were going home after our evening session, Sadiq queried us, "What is your opinion? I'm thinking about suggesting to Tahir that he divorce his wife Anwaar."

When Ismail asked why, he replied, "He didn't think ahead before racing into it, and so doubled his grief. Do you suppose a young woman of her age could live in that country without a heart?"

"Won't that suggestion just bring him more grief?"

"No—she's already left his life forever."

Sadiq revealed his thinking to Tahir on the following evening. The idea did not seem to surprise him.

"I've been considering that for a long time," he confessed. "It's only fair if she tries her luck again."

Tahir drew up a tender letter to her, conveying his request. Then came the divorce. We all heaved a sigh of relief. Yet it seemed to me that Tahir still wished for death, and was only waiting for it.

Ismail Qadri gave up the bar, waiting until he had earned retirement, then took his pension, in the time that the parties returned—the Wafd, in fact. His heart pounded and his old dreams inebriated him. Though now an old man with white hair, the new party was full of people with heads the same shade, some of them a decade or two older than himself.

"What is the message of the Wafd today?" asked Tahir Ubayd doubtfully.

"To defend democracy," he declared.

"To defend the free economy, then to get rid of the July Revolution," spat Tahir. "And to ensconce itself as the primary party of political reaction."

"It cannot neglect the demand for social justice, which it was the first to call for in its time," Ismail rejoined.

"That's what the National Party says," Tahir shot back. "Why establish two parties to realize the same message?"

Ismail kept on contemplating the subject, following the dialog between his head and his heart. But conditions forced the Wafd to freeze its activities, relieving him of his inner conflict.

With the passing of the days, Ismail woke us up both physically and mentally, and enamored us with continuous study. Tafida still clung to life despite the spread of old age from her body to her spirit, until she nearly forgot her émigré son. The greatest thing confronting the family at that time was the burden of survival, for despite Tafida's income plus Ismail's pension and his savings, they could not be certain to overcome inflation and preserve a reasonable standard of living.

Tafida owned a house that had fallen into ruin in Sabatiya: Sadiq suggested to Ismail that they sell it, benefiting from the rise in the price of land. Ismail convinced his wife to agree, and they sold it for fifty thousand pounds. This gave him a long period of tranquility that calmed and settled his heart, as he clear tendency toward spiritualism and Sufism dominated him. Ismail would quote the sayings of the great Sufis and expound on their symbols for us. He was alone in that, for no one responded to him or wanted to hear him. After all, Sadiq Safwan was a simple believer who did not approve of extravagant fantasies or symbolism. Hamada's hobby was moving back and forth, for he would be a Sufi one night, and the next would turn around and make fun of Ismail and all the authorities he cited.

As for Tahir, he had no religion at all.

"Are you a student who loves examining a subject, or do you just want to follow a path?" he jibed.

What a question to ask a man who had complete faith in the mind and knowledge and was unable to relinquish them.

"Intuition is a means to gain knowledge, like rational thinking, and each one has its place," answered Ismail.

"We know rational thinking quite intimately," Tahir replied dismissively. "But intuition is something we hear about only."

"We can know it too, as many have known it."

"We have to anticipate," Tahir barked contemptuously, "that one day he will come to us dressed in rags, turning against the world and all that's in it."

"No, I'm not one of those," Ismail riposted firmly. "The mystery is found in the world as it is found beyond it. The heaven, the earth, and all things proclaim it at all times. We have to be aware of what it tells us. I love the secret as it manifests itself in this world, just as I will adore its other existence after death."

"That is senility and fear of death," Tahir shrugged in scorn.

"It is love," said Ismail, smiling, "which is greater than old age and fear."

"How beautiful that you justify your attachment to this world in this way."

"Rather it is an attachment of a special kind," Ismail objected. "A sacred attachment, one not embarrassed to admit that the splendor of this world is concentrated in the woman."

Hamada al-Halawani broke out laughing at this.

"There's no need to twist and turn," he admonished. "Say you've entered your second adolescence. And that you're hatching a scheme to get entangled in marital betrayal."

"I must adorn myself with the virtue of patience," he said, smiling. Tahir then laughed as he had of old.

"You have shown us, Shaykh Ismail," he teased him, "that the shrines of your Sufi order are money, meditation, romance, and aphrodisiacs!"

In any case, Ismail's behavior did not provoke any fear in Tahir's imagination, at least not outwardly. With all his strength, he resisted regarding Ismail's actions as a form of escape, for Ismail did not turn away from life even at the final moment. Nor did he give up his love for it, or see it as finished. He did not surrender himself to contemplation until after he

112

had fulfilled his duty to the limit of his abilities over a long life. Nor did we see him having such clarity and sweetness before as we saw in him now. He did not hide behind appearances as Hamada did, for example. Rather, Ismail persuaded us that he had found in love what no ordinary lover discovered—and in sex what no average man could know.

Sadiq Safwan was right when he told us, "The police only know this behavior through a description in the Penal Code. May God protect him!"

We speed onward into our eighth decade, together. The corner in Qushtumur is still there—may Our Lord sustain it!—the sole stable thing, no matter the storms that rage around us. Her ancient walls do not come between ourselves and the world. The years rolling by so quickly do not stop our hearts from beating or tongues from talking. Even our forbearance gains from it, thanks to our shared memories and our long-standing affection. These are reinforced from time to time as we trade amusing tales with each other—or just a smile.

In fact, the inflation frightens us. The corruption worries us. The oppression upsets us. The day the leader was killed alarmed us, making us wonder what would come next. But despite old age, rheumatism, angina, prostate infection, and Sufism, we went, hobbling on canes, to the referendum center in the old school at Between the Gardens Street to elect the new president, to whom we'd attached our hopes. That is, as much as those hopes could be bound to life and belief.

Sadiq Safwan endured enormous pain from his rheumatism, yet his house was happy with the growing up of Nuha and her enrolling in preparatory school, and the visits of Ibrahim, Darya, and Nabila. The letters between him and Sabri, who pledged to come to Egypt for a stay with his family that he had created abroad, never ceased. Sadiq, in the meantime, had started to pray while sitting instead of kneeling and prostrating, spending time each day in the Sidi al-Kurdi mosque. Old age had descended upon him with a special beauty that burnished his head and mustache a gleaming white, and lent gravitas to his face.

"How will Nuha's and Nabila's time be?" he might have wondered.

The door opened to conversation about youth, the challenges of young people's reality today. And we talked of what the past had done to their present and their future.

"Your sons are luckier than the millions wasted," said Hamada al-Halawani.

"Perhaps the strain will melt them down and make giants out of them," commented Ismail Sadri.

"We have passed with our country through two revolutions, and have known both hopes and frustrations beyond number," Hamada digressed. "Are we to watch the nation ground up in an impasse that no one had ever imagined?"

"No one is absolved of their responsibility," answered Ismail. "We always err by putting the blame on one or two people."

So we put ourselves on trial, prolonged argument raging between defense and prosecution. Hamada was unable to defend himself. Then Sadiq spoke of his daughter Nuha, saying, "It pleases me that she's religious, but she's mad over western music, in love with television, and despite her academic supremacy, she does not love literary culture."

"She's become a Sufi with her own private order!" said Tahir with a guffaw.

"We've turned into walking skeletons," Sadiq said, staring into our aged faces. "It will be our misery to keep on living when the others have gone."

Hamada al-Halawani grew used to what vexed him. He was more patient and his complaints became rarer. The more time went by, the more he reconciled himself to life and was contented with it. He could no longer drive his car and thought of hiring a driver, but the cost gave him pause. So he parked the vehicle and took taxis instead.

"The rich of yesteryear have no worth now," he would tell us often.

Of the things Hamada savored in life, food and hashish remained, though he could no longer smoke the goza, the little hand-held water-pipe that he preferred. And he could not enjoy reading for more than two hours a day.

"It's only wise to assume," Sadiq Safwan was once heard to say, "that those among you who've sinned—even if to a tiny degree—have thought about what would happen to them in the afterlife."

His words did not go unnoticed by Hamada as they had by Tahir Ubayd. Hamada was not a complete stranger to belief. He had tried it as he had tried every opinion and conviction. He adopted Islam, then Christianity, and then the Jewish faith. For this reason he thought of what Sadiq said with interest. With the advent of Ramadan he decided to fast and pray, living as a Muslim for about a week, then renounced or forgot it, just as he had forgotten his angina. We almost forgot his illness along with him. When he had an attack of it, one of us took up the subject of our mortality.

"Anyone who torments himself at our age by being eager for life is mad," one of us smirked.

Sometimes his mind would wander, then he would say, "What a trick to swallow if we believe that our senses continue in the grave, even for a little while!"

"Have you regretted not having married or having children?" asked Sadiq Safwan.

"Absolutely not," he replied, "but I do regret my farcical experiment with being married."

Tahir Ubayd became greater both in wealth and loathing, while not losing weight. His illness did not exempt him from upset and disturbance from time to time. While he persisted in his desire for death, he nonetheless feared illness and its complications. News came to him that Anwaar Badran had married a colleague from the magazine: he informed us of this without flinching.

"How can you want to die," Sadiq Safwan grilled him, "when you have Darya and Nabila?"

"There's one human right missing: the right to die if one wants, using legal medicine with the method that provides the most ease."

Ismail Qadri went on his path from shrine to shrine, between reflection, love, and sex. His health remained strong in a miraculous way. As the days went by, he seemed five years younger than the rest of us, at least.

"Sexual potency has its limits, in any case," Tahir Ubayd reminded him.

"Maybe," Ismail answered confidently, "but the flowers, the stars, the night and the day remain with me. And don't forget this faithful corner in Qushtumur, the site of loyalty, affection, and honesty."

He let us know that his son Hebatallah had mentioned to him in his last letter that he was thinking about returning to Egypt to set up a suitable project. We were all happy to hear it.

※

The days rush on without stopping. They know neither pause nor rest. We grow older, and so does our love for each other. If one of us misses a night for a compelling reason, we are dismayed and disturbed. At the moments of the highest feeling, we hear the clanking of the wheels of time, while we see its fist clutching our final pages.

"I wonder how the end will come," pondered Hamada al-Halawani. "At home? On the road? In the coffeehouse? Mercifully easy or brutally hard?"

Quickly we fled into all other kinds of conversation.

Our memory rebelled against us all, not just against Hamada. He was discussing a topic one day when he forgot the name of the authority he wanted to cite.

"I mean the one who invented the theory of the monad," he sputtered when his power of recall failed him.

"Leibniz," Ismail remembered for him.

"How did his name escape me?" he wailed. "Will we have a second illiteracy at the end?"

We began to remember those whom forgetfulness had enfolded: Safwan al-Nadi and Zahrana Karim, Raafat Pasha al-Zayn and Zubayda Hanem Effat, Ihsan, Yusri Pasha al-Halawani and Afifa Hanem Nur al-Din, Ubayd Pasha al-Armalawi and Insaf Hanem al-Qulali, Qadri Suleiman and Fatiha Asal, plus dozens of colleagues and acquaintances.

Does any trace of the old Abbasiya remain? Where are the fields and the greenery? Where are the date palm and its council of kids, and the forest of Indian figs? Where are the houses with their hidden gardens? Where are the mansions, the palaces, and the aristocratic ladies? Do we see nothing today but jungles of reinforced concrete, and the turmoil of the madding crowd? Do we hear only racket and bedlam? Do only heaps of rubbish gaze back at us?

Whenever the news torments us, we delight in scurrying into the past to pluck its missing fruit. We do this despite our awareness of its deception and lies, knowing how the past is crammed with flaws and pains. Yet we are unable to resist enjoying this rich resource, filled with mirage and magic.

"I propose that we celebrate the passing of the seventy years of our sturdy friendship," said Sadiq Safwan one evening. We took this idea to our deepest hearts.

"Let's celebrate it in Khan al-Khalili," suggested Hamada.

"The houseboat is better," said Tahir Ubayd.

"Rather at Qushtumur," insisted Ismail Qadri, "for our friendship and Qushtumur cannot be rent asunder." We agreed to that without any debate. The place was filled with a humble party that befitted our age and state of health. We contented ourselves with the purchase of a cake, each taking a piece with our glasses of tea. We consigned what was left to the owner of the café, the waiters, and shoeshines. And we thought it proper that each of us said something appropriate to the occasion.

"I say, and I seek God's protection from envy and from those who envy," commenced Sadiq Safwan, "that seventy years have flowed by and not a single offense against our faithful friendship has slipped from any one of us, from near or far. So then, long may this pure feeling continue, and be an example to all the world."

"If we collected all the laughter that our worn-out hearts have drunk from the goblet of events," offered Hamada al-Halawani, "then it would fill an entire lake with sweet, pure water."

"Are we really fêting seventy years of friendship?" asked Tahir Ubayd. "Our country has passed through seven decades—but we have only lived through a minute together."

117

"History has enfolded what it has brought us," Ismail Qadri said in summary, "while our love remains new without end, forever."

I was about to summon the memory of the old rabab player when Sadiq Safwan woke me from my reverie as he chanted, with a clear and lucid voice:

> "*The Forenoon*
> *By the white forenoon*
> *and the brooding night!*
> *The Lord has neither forsaken thee nor hates thee*
> *and the Last shall be better for thee than the First.*
> *Thy Lord shall give thee, and thou shalt be satisfied.*
> *Did he not find you an orphan, and shelter thee?*
> *Did he not find you erring, and guide thee?*
> *Did he not find thee needy, and suffice thee?*
> *As for the orphan, do not oppress him,*
> *and as for the beggar, scold him not;*
> *and as for thy Lord's blessing, declare it.*"

Citation: al-Qur'an: Surat al-Duha, 93:1–11; translated by A.J. Arberry, *The Koran Interpreted* (New York: The Macmillan Company, 1955), p. 342.